GREAT ILLUSTRATED CLASSICS

GRIMM'S FAIRY TALES

adapted by Roy Nemerson

ABDO
Publishing Company

GREAT ILLUSTRATED CLASSICS

edited by
Joshua E. Hanft and Rochelle Larkin

visit us at
www.abdopub.com

Library edition published in 2005 by ABDO Publishing Company, 4940 Viking Drive, Suite 622, Edina, Minnesota 55435. Published by agreement with Playmore Incorporated Publishers and Waldman Publishing Corporation.

Printed in the United States.

Library of Congress Cataloging-in-Publication Data

Nemerson, Roy.
   Grimm's Fairy tales / adapted by Roy Nemerson ; edited by Joshua E. Hanft and Rochelle Larkin.
      p. cm. -- (Great illustrated classics)
   Contents: Sleeping Beauty -- Snow White -- The elves and the shoemaker -- Hansel and Gretel -- Rumpelstiltskin -- Little Red Riding Hood -- Rapunzel -- The golden goose -- The princess and the pea -- Cinderella -- Tom Thumb.
   ISBN 1-59679-241-8
   1. Fairy tales--Germany. [1. Fairy tales. 2. Folklore--Germany] I. Grimm, Wilhelm, 1786-1859. II. Grimm, Jacob, 1785-1863. III. Hanft, Joshua E. IV. Larkin, Rochelle. V. Kinder- und Hausmärchen. English. Selections. VI. Title. VII. Series.

PZ8.N35Gr 2005
[398.2]--dc22

2004062302

Contents

STORIES   PAGE

Sleeping Beauty 7

Snow White 29

The Elves and the Shoemaker 56

Hansel and Gretel 65

Rumpelstiltskin 101

Little Red Riding Hood 124

Rapunzel 142

The Golden Goose 161

The Princess and the Pea 184

Cinderella 196

Tom Thumb 221

About the Authors

Jacob and Wilhelm Grimm were brothers, born in Germany in the 1780's. While they were both well-educated and interested in many fields, it was the area of folklore that fascinated them most.

They wanted to preserve the heritage of stories that had been passed down from countless generations, but had never been written or published in any form, only told over and over again until there were many versions of the most popular tales.

The brothers tried to make their versions of the stories as accurate as possible. They worked very hard to hear as many stories as possible.

Although the stories were not originally meant especially for children, once the

Grimms' books were published, children all over the world began reading them—and never stopped! The characters brought to us by the Brothers Grimm include some of the best-loved figures in all of literature, and have appeared in many different ways, in film and television, as cartoons and picture books.

The brothers worked together almost all of their lives. The stories they collected for us have indeed been saved and loved, just as they wished.

The Seven Major Fairies of the Kingdom

Sleeping Beauty

Once upon a time a king and queen ruled a kingdom of many wonders. The royal couple was happy. But they'd have been much happier if they had a child.

They almost gave up hope of ever being parents when at last the queen gave birth to a baby girl. The king was so thrilled that he decreed the royal christening would take place in the castle to be followed by a great royal feast. The entire court and the seven major fairies of the kingdom were invited to attend.

The big day arrived. The castle was filled with its finest treasures. The grand dining hall was sparkling and all the castle servants were dressed in their best outfits.

After the christening in the chapel, everyone came into the dining hall and took their seats at the guest banquet tables.

"Look under your napkins. I have prepared a special gift for each of you," the king announced to the seven fairies.

The fairies all lifted their napkins. "How magnificent!" cried out one of the fairies. Indeed, for each of them had received a golden case. Inside each case were a knife, a fork, and a spoon, all made of diamonds and gold.

"I will treasure this gift for ever," the seventh and youngest fairy murmured.

"Where is my gift?" came a grumbling voice from the entrance way. Everyone turned. Standing in the entrance was an old, ugly-looking woman.

"Who is that?" the king asked.

"She's an old fairy," one of the fairies replied.

A Grumbling Voice from the Entrance

"But no one has seen her in over fifty years. It's rumored she lives alone in her castle with no one but bats and snakes for company."

The king motioned to the old woman. "I don't have any more gold boxes, but you are welcome to join us in our feast."

"No gold box for me," the old crone mumbled. "Then I promise something wicked will befall your little baby."

The only one to hear those words mumbled was the youngest fairy. She was frightened by them, but decided to wait and see what happened.

"It is now time for us to give our gifts to the baby princess," the first fairy said. "My gift is for her to be the most beautiful girl in the whole world."

"I am giving her the goodness of an angel," the second fairy said.

"My gift is to bestow grace on everything she does," the third fairy said.

"I shall give her the gift of dance," the fourth fairy said.

The fifth fairy said, "I give her the most perfect singing voice in the kingdom."

"I guarantee she will be able to play every musical instrument perfectly," the sixth fairy said.

Before the seventh and youngest fairy could offer her gift, the ugly old fairy stood up. "I have a gift to give," she said. "I give her death!" Everyone gasped. "I predict a needle will pierce her skin, causing her to bleed, and killing her right away."

Everyone began to shout at the old fairy. The king and queen began to cry. The seventh fairy then held up her hand.

"Wait!" the seventh fairy called out. "I, too, have a gift. Now, I cannot prevent a needle from piercing your daughter's skin. But I promise you she will not die. She will, instead, sleep for one hundred years. After one hundred years, a handsome young prince will come to her, kiss her, and she will awake. She and the prince will then live a happy life together."

At that point the feast ended. The fairies all

The Princess Grew into a Beautiful Girl.

returned to their parts of the kingdom. The ugly old fairy returned to her creepy castle and was not seen again.

Meanwhile, the king decided to take action. He ordered that all spindles and sewing needles be banned from the kingdom. He decreed that anyone caught with a needle would be instantly put to death. All the spinning wheels in the kingdom were destroyed. No more needles were to be seen.

The king's decree seemed to work. Some years passed, and the baby princess had grown into a beautiful girl. She had never seen or come near a sewing needle or spindle.

One day the king and queen went to visit a royal couple in a nearby kingdom. While her parents were away, the princess decided to explore different parts of the castle she had never seen.

The princess had not been to the very top tower of the castle. She ran lightly up the stairs. At the top of the stairs, she saw a door. She knocked on it. "Come in," called a voice.

The princess entered. A little old lady was sitting in a chair. Next to her was an odd-looking object.

"What is that thing?" the princess asked, stepping closer.

"This is a spindle, young lady," the woman said. "I am making warm cloth for the coming winter."

The old woman had never heard about the king's decree forbidding spindles and needles. Nor did she know that the young lady before her was the royal princess.

"That looks wonderful," the princess said. "May I try it?"

"You may," the woman replied. "But be careful, these needles are sharp."

The old woman handed the princess the needle. The old woman's hand shook. She accidentally pierced the princess's pinky with the sharp needle. The princess's finger began to bleed. The princess instantly closed her eyes and fell to the floor.

"Help!" the old woman shrieked. In only a

"This Is a Spindle."

moment, servants and guards appeared in the room. When they saw the princess lying unconscious, they started to rub her forehead. They poured cold water on her hands. They tried everything. But nothing would awaken the princess.

Within the hour the king and queen returned home. When they heard the news, they raced upstairs to the old woman's room. The king ordered the princess be taken to a special chamber and placed on an enormous bed.

"It's happened," the queen said, sobbing. "Our little girl will sleep for a hundred years. We'll never talk to her again!"

The king stared down at his daughter, lying under the covers of the bed. The princess looked beautiful. Her cheeks were rosy red. Her hair was blond and shining. She was breathing peacefully. "She is resting in peace," the king said with a deep sigh. "That is the best we can hope for."

Soon the news of the princess's condition

reached the seventh, youngest fairy. The fairy jumped into her chariot, led by a team of dragons, and raced off to the castle.

When she arrived at the castle, the fairy was led into the princess's room by the king and queen. "You have done all you can," the fairy said. "She will sleep just like this for one hundred years, until her prince awakens her. But we must prepare her for that moment."

The fairy knew when the princess awoke she would need people around to help her. So the fairy went throughout the castle, tapping everyone with her magic wand. Each person she tapped instantly fell asleep.

The fairy tapped servants, guards, chefs, footmen, ladies-in-waiting, stewards and maids. Some fell asleep standing up, others slumped into chairs, or dropped softly to the floor. But all were sound asleep. The fairy even tapped several horses and the princess's pet dog. The animals all fell into a peaceful sleep.

"What about us?" the queen asked. "Can't the king and I be put to sleep, so when our

"So Long a Sleep"

daughter awakens we will be with her?"

"No," the fairy answered gently. "You are royal leaders, and you have an obligation to your subjects. I cannot place you into so long a sleep."

Sadly, the king and queen kissed their sleeping daughter good-bye. Tears ran down their cheeks as they whispered farewell to the princess. It was farewell because the king ordered all those still awake to leave the castle.

"This castle is to remain closed to all visitors until that time a hundred years from now when the prince arrives," the king announced. The king and queen then got into a carriage, and were driven off, to live the remainder of their lives in another castle.

As soon as the king and queen left, an amazing thing happened. The trees, bushes and brambles growing nearby suddenly grew closely together and completely surrounded the castle. It became impossible for anyone to get near.

Only the topmost tower of the castle was visible, and that could only be seen from a hill in the distance.

Many years passed, and the castle remained closed. Nobody came near it; nobody entered. As new generations were born and grew older, rumors about the castle spread. Some said it was haunted. Others said a devil lived inside it. The sleeping princess was all but forgotten.

Then, one day, a handsome young prince from a nearby kingdom went out for a day's ride. He brought his horse to a stop on top of a hill for a drink of water. He noticed the chimney top of the castle.

"What is that?" the young prince asked one of his elderly advisors.

"My lord, it is said that is a haunted castle," the advisor replied. "It is rumored something dreadful happened there a hundred years ago, that a beautiful princess sleeps within, and waits to be awakened by a brave and handsome prince."

"Really?" replied the prince. He had been

Out for a Day's Ride

thinking that he had never been in love. He had yet to find the perfect princess for him. This story of a beautiful sleeping princess set his mind and soul on fire. "I think I'll go see this princess for myself," the prince said.

"My lord, that is not wise. It is also said that the castle is haunted by demons," the advisor pleaded. But the prince was brave and valiant. Honor and romance led him to the castle.

As the prince approached an amazing thing happened. The trees, bushes and brambles that had been surrounding and protecting the castle, suddenly parted. The prince slipped off his horse and entered the castle grounds.

The moment he did, the trees, bushes and brambles again surrounded the castle. None of the prince's advisors could come with him. He was alone. But he was a brave prince, and feared nothing.

He entered the courtyard. The prince stared in silence. Everywhere he looked, people and animals lay or stood, with eyes closed. They were clearly sleeping, not dead. The people looked healthy, the animals looked hardy. All were breathing easily.

The prince continued on, and entered the castle. Again, he saw many healthy looking people, all sound asleep. The prince climbed a flight of stairs. He found himself standing before a wide doorway. The prince entered the room.

It was an elegant chamber. The prince let out a short gasp. Lying on a bed was the most beautiful girl the prince had ever seen. She, too, was sleeping.

He slowly, carefully approached. The closer the prince got, the more beautiful he could see she was. With a slight trembling in his knees, the prince stood by the bed.

He leaned over, and gently kissed the princess on the top of her forehead.

Instantly, her eyes fluttered and opened. The prince stared into the two most beautiful blue eyes he had ever seen. The princess smiled at him. "Is it you, my prince?" she asked softly. "I have waited for you all this while."

"I Never Dreamed of So Handsome a Prince."

The prince was enchanted by these words. He knelt by the bed and they began to talk. The princess spoke of the many dreams she had had these past hundred years. "But I never dreamed so handsome a prince would come and awaken me," she said.

The prince smiled. "I have been looking for my true love all my life," he replied. "I never dreamed I would find her sleeping in a castle."

"Do you love me?" asked the princess. The prince assured her he loved her more than his own life.

They talked much more. Meanwhile, all around them, the people and animals in the castle were also waking up. People began attending to their jobs and duties. The princess's dog came running into the chamber and leaped on her bed, licking her face. The princess laughed, and hugged her pet.

The prince was telling the princess of all the things that had happened in the world the past hundred years, when a lady-in-waiting entered the chamber.

"Your grace, lunch is served," the lady-in-waiting announced.

"I am coming," the princess replied, "for I have not eaten in so long a time."

The princess climbed out of bed and stood up.

The prince stared at her.

"What is the matter?" the princess asked.

"You are the most beautiful girl in the world," the prince replied. "But you are dressed in the clothes my great-great-great-grandmother wore."

" I will soon learn the fashions of today," the princess replied happily.

"It doesn't matter," the prince said with a happy sigh. "Whatever you wear, you will make look wonderful."

Then he took her hand in his. Together they went to the dining hall. They sat at the large table. All around them servants, musicians, guards and attendants who hadn't been awake in one hundred years were suddenly back at work.

He Took Her Hand in His.

All the castle had come back to life, and it was as if the princess never slept at all. But oh, she was so very hungry, she told the prince as a fitting feast was prepared and brought to them from the once again bustling kitchens of the castle.

As the music played, the loving couple ate their first meal together. Soon after, they went into the royal chapel. The wedding ceremony was performed and they lived happily ever after for the rest of their lives.

Snow White

Once upon a time in a northern kingdom, it was the middle of winter. Snowflakes were falling like thick feathers. The lovely queen of the realm was sitting inside her chamber, sewing near an ebony black window. She accidentally pricked her finger with the needle. Three drops of royal blood fell onto the white linen, white as the snow just outside the window.

The queen stared out at the snow and the dark night. "I wish I had a daughter with skin

Her Wish Soon Came True.

white as snow, blood-red cheeks and dark-as-night black hair," she thought to herself.

Being a queen, her wish soon came true. She gave birth to a daughter with skin white as snow, with blood-red cheeks and beautiful black hair. The queen named her baby Snow White. Unfortunately, soon after, the good queen became ill and died.

The king grieved for his dead wife. But within a short time, to ease his grief, he re-married. His new wife was quite beautiful, but she was very selfish and vain. She always insisted on being the most beautiful woman in the room.

She even had a magic mirror to help her. She would stand before the mirror, look at her reflection, and demand:

"Mirror, mirror on the wall
Who's the fairest one of all?"
The mirror always replied:
"You, my Queen, are the fairest."

This would make the queen happy, for she knew the mirror was forbidden to lie.

The vain queen, however, became aware that the king's daughter, Snow White, was growing into a very beautiful young girl. One day the queen went to her magic mirror and asked it who was the fairest of all.

This time, the mirror replied:

"You, my Queen, have a beauty most rare

But Snow White is a thousand times more fair."

The queen was enraged and filled with envy. "How dare that little girl be the most fair. I will put an end to this at once!" the evil queen said.

She summoned a huntsman to her chambers. "Take the girl out into the woods, kill her, and bring back her heart to prove to me she's dead. Now hurry!"

The huntsman led Snow White into the middle of the woods. He suddenly pulled out his knife and was about to stab the little girl when Snow White dropped to her knees, crying.

"Huntsman, please don't kill me," Snow White sobbed. "If you let me live, I'll run away into the woods. You'll never see me again."

The Queen and Her Magic Mirror

The huntsman pitied this beautiful young girl. "Very well, you may go," he said. He thought Snow White wouldn't last long alone in the forest. He watched as she dashed off into the trees.

At that instant a wild boar came charging at the huntsman. He stabbed the beast to death. Then he removed its heart and brought it back to the queen. The queen was pleased.

Meanwhile, Snow White was all alone in the wild forest. Fierce animals charged by in all directions. She ran for as long and as fast as she could. Suddenly, she came to a small cottage in a clearing.

Snow White went in. Everything in the cottage was tiny. It was all clean and neat, but tiny. There was a tiny table and everything on it was tiny too—the cups, the plates, the forks and spoons. Snow White counted seven small seats at the table.

Then she noticed seven little beds in a corner of the room. By now she was very hungry and tired. She ate some food from each of the seven tiny plates, and drank some cider from each of the seven tiny cups.

Then sleep began to overtake her. She tried each of the beds, but not until the seventh one did she find one that fit her. She climbed into the bed, said her prayers, and went to sleep.

In the middle of the dark night, seven little men entered the cottage. They lived there, and had been out all day in the mountains, mining for gold. As they put their picks and shovels away, they noticed that their cottage looked different.

"Who's been sitting in my chair?" asked the first dwarf.

"Who's been eating my bread?" asked the second.

"Who's been eating off my plate?" asked the third.

"Who's been eating my vegetables?" asked the fourth.

"Who's been using my fork?" asked the fifth.

"Who's been cutting with my knife?" asked the sixth.

They Did Not Wake Her Up.

"Who's been drinking from my cup?" asked the seventh.

Then they noticed that their beds were all rumpled. As the dwarfs talked this over, the seventh dwarf suddenly saw Snow White, sleeping in his bed. "There's someone in my bed!" he shouted.

The others came running over. They all lit tiny candles and stared at the sleeping girl.

They were so pleased to have such a beautiful child in their cottage, that they did not wake her up. Instead, they went to sleep, with the seventh dwarf sleeping in a chair.

The next morning, Snow White woke up. When she saw the seven dwarfs, her first thought was to run away, because they looked so strange.

"Don't be frightened," one of the dwarfs said. "We like you. We won't hurt you. What's your name?"

"Snow White," she replied. She told them the story of her jealous stepmother, the huntsman, and how she had found their cottage.

"You can stay here with us, and you'll be safe. In exchange, you can cook, sew, clean and make our beds," the eldest dwarf said.

"I accept," Snow White replied. She knew now she would be safe.

From that day on, the dwarfs would go off each morning to the mountain, in search of gold and jewels. When they returned each night, Snow White would have dinner ready for them, and the cottage would be clean and snug.

But one of the dwarfs had a warning for Snow White. "Your evil stepmother may learn that you're here," he said. "So you must be sure never to let anyone into the cottage when you are alone."

At that very moment the stepmother was standing before her magic mirror. She asked it:

"Mirror, mirror on the wall
Who in this realm is fairest of all?"

The mirror immediately replied:

"You, my queen, have a beauty quite rare
But in the mountains, where the seven

Now She Would Be Safe.

dwarfs dwell
Snow White is thriving, and this I must tell:
Within this realm she's still the most fair."

The queen was outraged. Since the mirror could not lie, this meant the huntsman hadn't killed the girl and she was still alive.

She needed a new plan. This time she would finish off Snow White by herself. She couldn't trust anyone else to do it. So the queen made herself up to look like an old, poor peddler woman.

Then she went out into the woods, and climbed through the mountains, until she came to the dwarfs' cottage. She knocked on the door, crying out, "Pretty things for sale, pretty things!"

Snow White looked out the window. It was during the day, so she was all alone. But this poor old woman certainly looked harmless.

"What kind of things do you have?" Snow White called back.

"Pretty things," the disguised queen replied. "Laces and ribbons for you to wear."

Snow White wanted some new ribbons, so she unlatched the door and let the woman in.

"Try one of these ribbons," the stepmother said. "Here, let me help you."

The evil woman helped Snow White with a ribbon. But she tied it so tightly that Snow White was unable to breathe. She fell to the floor.

"Now I will be the fairest in the realm, once and for all," the evil stepmother said. She left the cottage, and headed back to the castle.

That night, the seven dwarfs returned to the cottage. When they saw Snow White lying on the floor, they feared she was dead. She wasn't moving and she seemed not to be breathing.

"Quick, cut that ribbon," one of the dwarfs said. They cut, and it fell off, and instantly Snow White began to breathe. Soon, she totally revived. She told them the story of the old peddler woman.

"That wasn't an old peddler woman," one of

Off to Work

the dwarfs said. "That was your evil step-mother, the queen. You must be careful, Snow White. Let no one into the cottage while we're gone." Then off they went to work.

By now the stepmother had returned to the castle. She went right to the magic mirror, and asked it:

"Mirror, mirror on the wall
Who in this realm is fairest of all?"

The mirror replied:

"You, my queen, have a beauty quite rare
But in the mountains, where the seven
    dwarfs dwell
Snow White is thriving, and this I must
    tell:
Within this realm, she's still the most
    fair."

"She's not dead!" the queen screamed. "I will kill that girl even if it means I have to lose my own life!" She immediately ran into a secret chamber of the castle. She mixed together many potions and liquids until she had created the deadliest poison ever invented.

Then the evil queen took an apple and painted the outside with the deadly poison. The apple looked delicious. It had a shiny white and red skin. But anyone who bit into the poisoned part of the apple would die instantly.

Then the queen again disguised herself. This time she dressed herself to look like a peasant. She left the castle, went through the mountains, and arrived at the cottage of the seven dwarfs.

She knocked on the front door. Snow White poked her head out of the window and saw a peasant woman standing there. "What is it you want?" Show White asked.

"I'm selling apples," the disguised queen replied. She held up the poisoned apple. "They're quite delicious. May I come in and show you?"

"I'm not allowed to let anyone in the cottage when I'm alone," Snow White replied.

"You have nothing to fear," the evil queen replied. "Do you think that the apple might be

The Apple Looked Delicious.

poisoned? I assure you it's not. Look." The queen then cut the apple in two. "I'll eat the white part, and you can eat the red," she said. The evil queen bit into the white part. Snow White couldn't know that only red half of the apple had been poisoned.

Snow White watched as the disguised queen ate the white half. The queen swallowed and smiled. "See? I'm fine. It is really delicious."

Snow White couldn't resist, the apple looked so good. "I'll try the red half," she said. The queen handed Snow White the rest of the apple through the window. Snow White bit into it. Two seconds later Snow White fell to the floor. She was dead.

The evil queen laughed. Then she turned and fled back to her castle. When she got home she raced to the mirror.

"Mirror, mirror, on the wall
Now who's the fairest one of all?"
The mirror immediately replied:
"Of all the realm that can be seen
You are the fairest one, my queen."

The evil queen breathed a sigh of relief. Her plan had worked. Snow White was finally dead, and the jealous queen was again the most beautiful woman in the entire kingdom.

That evening, the seven dwarfs returned to the cottage. They were shocked to find Snow White lying on the floor. They quickly threw water on her, loosened her clothes, and tried everything they could think of to revive her. But nothing worked. Snow White was dead.

The sad dwarfs lifted Snow White and placed her bed outside. They sat and cried for three whole days. They couldn't believe their beautiful young friend was dead. For even in death, Snow White's cheeks had a rosy red glow.

"We can't bury her in the ground," one of the dwarfs said. "She is much too beautiful to lie in the ground."

So the dwarfs built a coffin made of glass. They placed Snow White inside. They wrote a message saying that a royal princess lay in this coffin.

The Dwarfs Took Turns.

The grieving dwarfs carried the coffin to the top of a nearby mountain. The dwarfs placed the coffin in an open spot, for all to see. Many animals came by to mourn for Snow White, including a deer, an owl, a raven and a dove. They all wept for Snow White.

She remained in the glass coffin, on top of the mountain, for many years. Though she was dead, she continued to look the same. Her skin was white as snow, her cheeks were a rosy red, and her hair was long and black, as her own mother had wished her to be.

The dwarfs would all take turns guarding Snow White's coffin, for they cared for her so much.

One evening, as the dwarfs were finishing dinner, a prince knocked on the door of their cottage. "May I spend the night with you? It is getting late and I need a place to stay," the prince asked. The friendly dwarfs allowed the prince to stay in their cottage for the night.

The next morning the dwarfs took the prince up the mountain to show him Snow White's coffin. The prince read the message, proclaiming Snow White a princess.

"She is lovely," he said to the dwarfs. "Please let me care for this coffin and this beautiful princess, and cherish her forever, for I love her as if she were alive."

The dwarfs were so moved by the prince's words that they took great pity on him. They agreed to let him take Snow White's coffin.

The prince summoned his servants to the top of the mountain and ordered them to carry the coffin down. The servants lifted the coffin, but as they started down the mountain trail, one of them tripped, and dropped the coffin.

The coffin hit the ground with a jolt. It hit so hard that the poisonous piece of apple flew out of Snow White's mouth.

In moments, Snow White opened her eyes and sat up. The stunned prince opened the top of the coffin.

"You are alive!" shouted the prince.

"Yes, I am," Snow White replied, looking around. "But where am I?"

"You Are Alive!" Shouted the Prince.

"You are on top of a mountain with a prince who loves you deeply," the prince replied. He then explained to Snow White about the poisoned apple and all that had happened. Snow White was very grateful to be alive.

"I am so happy you are alive," the prince said. "I would be even happier if you would become my wife. Will you marry me?"

Snow White smiled at the prince. "Yes, I will, for I love you as truly as you love me," she said.

They went off to the royal castle, and soon after their wedding was held, with great pomp and pageantry.

Snow White's evil stepmother had been invited to the wedding. After she had gotten herself all dressed up for the wedding, the bad queen went back to her mirror and asked:

"Mirror, mirror on the wall
Who in this realm is fairest of all?"

The mirror replied:

"You, my queen, have a beauty quite rare
But Snow White is a thousand times
more fair."

The evil queen almost fainted. Snow White was alive! How was this possible? She was so upset at this news she didn't want to go to the wedding. But she had promised the king and queen she would attend, so she went off.

When the evil queen arrived at the prince's castle, she entered the main hall. Snow White and her prince were standing, greeting the guests.

The evil queen took one look and recognized Snow White. She was astonished. How could this be happening? How was Snow White alive and looking so beautiful?

But before the queen could ask any questions, a servant brought over a tray. On the tray were a pair of red-hot iron slippers.

"You are requested to put on these slippers and dance." The evil queen slipped the burning slippers onto her feet and began to dance. The slippers were so hot, and the pain they caused so great, that the evil queen fell to the floor. She was dead.

Snow White and Her Prince Danced.

The evil queen, who had tried so hard to kill Snow White, was herself gone, and all her wicked ways were gone with her. Nobody was really sorry about it. She had worked all her bad magic against the pretty little princess.

But Snow White and her prince danced and laughed, and lived happily ever after.

The Elves and the Shoemaker

Once upon a time in a small village there lived a poor little shoemaker and his wife. He was so poor that he had just enough leather left to make one pair of shoes.

So he carefully cut out the shoes, placed them on his work table, and decided he would finish working on them the next morning. He got into bed, said his prayers, and fell fast asleep.

The next morning the shoemaker awoke bright and early. He got out of bed, went over

Finished the Next Morning

to his table, and got ready to finish stitching the shoes.

He froze in place. He stared at the table. He couldn't believe what he saw. The two shoes were all made. They were sitting on the table, all their leather stitches in place.

"How could this have happened?" the shoemaker asked his wife, as they picked the shoes up and examined them. They were perfect. In fact, they were the best made pair of shoes ever seen!

Moments later there was a knock on the door. "Come in," the shoemaker called out. A customer entered.

"I'm looking for a new pair of shoes," the customer said. The shoemaker held up the shoes.

"Those are magnificent," the customer said. "How much do they cost?"

The shoemaker gave a price, much more than he had ever asked for a pair of shoes before. To his great joy, the customer paid the price and took the shoes with him.

Using this money, the shoemaker bought

more leather. He bought enough to make two pairs of shoes. That evening he cut out the shoes, placed them on the table, and decided he'd finish them in the morning. He got into bed, said his prayers, and fell asleep.

The next morning, to the shoemaker's astonishment, two pairs of perfectly stitched shoes were sitting on his table! Before lunch the shoemaker had sold both pairs. He now had enough money to buy leather to make four pairs of shoes!

He again cut out the shoes, left them on his table, and went to bed for the night. The next morning, when he awoke there were four perfectly stitched pairs of shoes standing on the table!

The shoemaker continued to do this for many more nights. Each night he would leave the cut leather on his table. Each morning he would find the shoes already perfectly stitched. Each day he would sell the shoes, and make more money.

Soon the shoemaker found he had quite a lot

He'd Never Seen Such Fast Work.

of money. The timing was perfect, because Christmas was coming. The shoemaker turned to his wife and said, "Why don't we stay up all night tonight, and see who it is who's making the shoes for us?"

"Sounds like a good idea," his wife replied. So she lit a candle, and the two of them hid behind some coats hanging against the wall.

At exactly midnight, two short little elves came into the room through the window. They immediately sat down at the work table. They picked up the leather the shoemaker had left on the table, and they began to stitch, hammer and sew.

The shoemaker watched in total shock. He'd never seen such fast work in his life. In a short period of time, the two elves finished making all the shoes, and they quickly scampered out of the window and were gone.

The shoemaker and his wife went to sleep. The next morning at breakfast, the wife said, "Those little elves have made us rich. They were wearing very thin clothing. It is so cold out. Why don't we show them our gratitude and buy them some clothes for Christmas? I can get them some shirts, jackets and trousers. I could also knit some stockings for them, and you could make them each a pair of shoes."

The shoemaker agreed. By early that evening, all the gifts were ready. The shoemaker and his wife placed the gifts on the workbench near the table. Then they again hid themselves and waited for the elves.

At exactly midnight, the two elves came in through the window and raced over to the work table. The elves were about to sit down and begin stitching shoes, when they saw the gifts.

At first they were confused. There was no shoe leather on the table. Then they realized these gifts must be meant for them.

They immediately opened the boxes. The elves were thrilled! They put on all the clothes and began to dance around the room, singing:

"This is swell, this is fun

We have new clothes, and our work is done."

The elves scampered back out the window,

They Put on All the Clothes.

and were never seen or heard from again. The shoemaker and his wife continued to prosper, however, and lived happily ever after.

They often thought about the mysterious little men who had done so much to help them, and had disappeared as suddenly as they had come. They were glad that they had been able to do something for their happy little helpers and promised that they would always help others whenever they could.

Hansel and Gretel

Once upon a time, in a forest far, far away, there lived a father, a mother and their two children. The boy was named Hansel and his younger sister was named Gretel. Their real mother had died a few years before. Their father had re-married, and so the woman in the house was actually Hansel and Gretel's stepmother.

The forest was lonely, dark, and kind of scary. Hansel and Gretel had very few neighbors, and practically no friends. In fact, their

But Hansel Could Still Hear.

best friend was their white cat, Snowy.

One night, while Hansel and Gretel were playing with Snowy in their small bedroom, they could hear their father and stepmother talking loudly, through the wall.

"What are they talking about?" Gretel asked.

"Wait here, I'll go and see," Hansel said. Hansel left the room quietly. In the hallway he could see the door to his parents' room was closed. But he could still hear.

"You're not making very much money chopping wood this year," the stepmother said. "We barely have enough food to last the week."

"The whole territory is suffering," the father replied. "Everyone is having trouble getting enough to eat. There's been a drought and the famine is everywhere."

"But not everyone has two useless little mouths to feed like we do," the stepmother said angrily. "If Hansel and Gretel were gone, you and I would have enough food."

Hansel's blue eyes went wide as he heard these words spoken by his stepmother. Was she saying she wanted to get rid of him and his sister?

"Here's my plan," the stepmother continued. "Tomorrow morning we take them out into the deep woods. We'll build a fire, give them a few slices of bread, and then tell them we'll be back to get them after you've chopped down some trees. But we won't return. And that's the last we'll see of them."

"I can't do that!" the father shouted. "You're asking me to leave my children to the beasts of the forests. Wild animals will kill and eat them as soon as night falls. Their real mother would never let that happen!"

"Well, if we don't do it, then we'll all starve to death very soon. What's better, all four of us dying, or the two of us staying alive?"

Father fell silent. Hansel realized his stepmother had tricked his father into agreeing with her. Hansel quickly hurried back to his room and told Gretel what he had heard.

Gretel began to cry. "We'll be eaten alive before midnight tomorrow," she whimpered.

Gretel Began to Cry.

"No, we won't let it happen," Hansel said, putting his arm around his trembling sister's shoulder. "I promise you, we'll be all right."

Soon the candle went out and their room grew dark. Gretel climbed into her bed. Snowy jumped onto the bed, and cuddled in her arms. "Aren't you going to sleep?" Gretel whispered to her brother.

"In a few minutes," Hansel replied. "I have something to do first."

Hansel crept out of the room. His parents' room was dark. They were both asleep. Hansel tip-toed to the front door, opened it, and stepped outside.

It was cool. The moon was nearly full and shone brightly over the forest. An owl hooted in a nearby tree, causing Hansel to jump. Then a wolf howled in the distance.

Hansel quickly went about his work. He scooped up little white pebbles from the ground and stuffed them into his pockets. Then he went back into the house, closed the door, and returned to his room.

Gretel had been unable to fall asleep. "Hansel, what were you doing?" she asked.

"Don't worry, Gretel. Like I said, we're going to be all right."

The next morning as the sun dawned, the stepmother noisily banged on the childrens' door. "Wake up, you two!" she cried. "We're going into the forest to fetch some wood."

Hansel and Gretel looked at each other, but said nothing. They knew what their step-mother's plan was.

Soon the four of them were walking along the trail leading from their house into the forest. Hansel stopped to look behind him. "What are you doing, looking backwards?" the step-mother shouted. "We're moving ahead!"

"I just wanted to wave at Snowy. He's on the roof of the house," Hansel said.

"You're a very stupid boy," she said. "That's not your silly cat, that's the sun shining off the roof. Now let's keep moving!"

But Hansel hadn't been looking at the house or Snowy. He had been looking back to see the

The Trail of White Pebbles

trail of white pebbles he had been dropping along the way. He smiled at Gretel, and the four of them continued on into the forest.

After about an hour they had reached the middle of the forest. There were no houses or people about, only the narrow path and many trees, most of them with wilted or dying leaves. The drought had affected the trees very badly.

"Your father and I are going to see about chopping down some trees," the stepmother said. "You children wait for us here. Build a fire and eat this bread. We'll be back in about an hour."

The stepmother handed Gretel a small loaf of bread.

"Father, are you sure you'll be safe by yourselves in the deep forest?" Hansel asked.

The father turned and stared at his son. "Yes, I'll be just fine," he said softly. "You two take care," he said, kissing Gretel on the forehead and rubbing Hansel's shoulder.

"Hurry or we'll lose the sunlight!" the stepmother snarled. Soon the two adults were gone into the woods.

"Father looked so sad," Gretel said. "He knows he'll never see us again." She began to cry softly.

"He'll see us again," Hansel said. "Let's have some bread. I'm starving."

The two of them quickly ate up the small loaf. Then they gathered some sticks, made a fire, and laid back against some rocks as the fire's glow kept them warm.

Suddenly, in the distance, came a sharp, thudding sound.

"That must be Father chopping down a tree," Hansel said. "Maybe he'll gather enough wood so they won't have to abandon us after all. Let's go see!"

Hansel and Gretel put out the fire, then went into the woods. They ran through the trees, ducking under limbs and branches. The thudding noise grew louder and louder.

"Father, Father, here we are!" Gretel called out. Suddenly she and Hansel stopped dead in their tracks.

The Fire's Glow Kept Them Warm.

The thudding noise was right in front of them. It wasn't being made by an axe cutting a tree. It was a dead branch that had been tied to a tree trunk, banging against it, making the sound.

"They did this to make us think they were here. They probably left hours ago," Gretel said. She looked around. "Now we're lost. I don't know this part of the forest."

"It's alright," Hansel said. "Just wait until the moon comes out."

A few hours later, after the sun had set and the air grew dark and cool, the moon popped into the night sky. It covered the ground with a white glow. "See, there's our way out!" Hansel cried.

Sure enough, the white pebbles he had dropped along the way gleamed like bright little lights in the ground. Hansel and Gretel followed the trail of pebbles, and after several hours they were standing in front of their house, safely home.

"We're home!" Gretel shrieked as she and

her brother bounded into the house. The stepmother was baking a small loaf of bread. Father was sharpening his axe.

"Oh children, you're home!" he cried, rushing to hug them. The stepmother just glared. "You bad children," she said. "Why did you stay in the forest so long? Your father and I were scared to death."

"Sorry," Hansel said, staring back. "I guess we lost track of time."

Life returned to normal. Food remained scarce and the stepmother continued to urge the father to get rid of the children. He pleaded with her that this was a cruel thing to do. He knew he would be forced to try it again.

What the parents didn't know was that Hansel was wise to their ways. So every night, before bedtime, he would stand outside his parents' bedroom and listen through the door.

"Tomorrow we'll take them even further into the forest," the stepmother said. "This time we'll make sure they don't return."

Hansel ran back into his room. Gretel was

It Had Been Bolted and Locked.

holding Snowy. "They're going to leave us again tomorrow in the forest," Hansel said.

"It's time for a pebble search again, then," Gretel said, smiling. Hansel nodded. He went to the front door. But it had been bolted and locked. There was no way to get out!

Hansel turned and went back to their room. He told Gretel what had happened. Gretel began to tremble again. "Without the white pebbles, we'll be lost. We'll never get home. We'll be killed!" she cried.

"Sshh!" Hansel said, holding his finger to his lips. "Something good will turn up. I just know it. You must have trust. And faith."

Gretel stopped trembling. She and Hansel got into their beds and tried to fall asleep. But sleep came hard that night, because the next day held many fears for them.

Early in the morning, their stepmother banged on the door with a broom. "Up, up, you lazybones!" she growled. "We're going back into the woods. Here are a few slices of bread, but keep them for lunch. You'll need them then."

The family again headed down the path, into the woods, away from their house. Hansel turned, and looked back at the house.

"Why are you stopping, boy?" the stepmother demanded. "Why do you keep looking back at the house?"

"I thought I saw Snowy jumping out of the chimney," Hansel said.

"You're blind as a bat!" the stepmother said. "That's just some soot blowing. Now move along or we'll be late!"

What the others couldn't see was that Hansel was dropping small bits of crumbs from his bread onto the trail. He looked down and saw the crumbs, which led back to their house. He winked at Gretel, and they continued on.

They walked for many miles, going deeper into the woods than ever before. Suddenly they stopped. "This will do," the stepmother said. "Your father and I have much wood chopping to do. You sit here and wait for us. If you get tired, take a nap. But whatever you do, you are not to leave until we come back for you. Do you

Hansel Was Dropping Crumbs.

understand?"

Hansel and Gretel nodded. "Good-bye, Father," Gretel said, hugging him.

"Good-bye, my sweetness," the father replied, hugging his little girl.

The stepmother pulled the father away. Soon father and stepmother were out of sight.

"I'm really hungry," Hansel said. "But I dropped all my bread along the path."

"You can share mine," Gretel said. She broke her pieces in half, and gave half to her brother. They ate their bread quickly. They lay back in the golden sun that shone through the trees. Soon they grew sleepy. Their eyes closed.

Hansel suddenly jerked awake. He looked around. Hours had passed. Nightfall had come. There was no sign of their parents. He tapped Gretel on the shoulder. She awoke with a start.

"We're alone," he said. "It's dark. We've got to start back."

"The moon's out," Gretel said. "It should make it easy to see the bread crumbs."

But there was one problem. There were no

bread crumbs on the path. Hungry animals and birds had eaten up all the crumbs!

Hansel spotted some berries growing on the ground. He swiftly picked them, cleaned them off, and he and Gretel ate them all up.

Then they started to wander off, hoping to find the trail to lead them out of the deep woods and back to their home.

Hours passed. The night slowly turned to dawn. No animals had attacked them. But they were growing weaker and weaker. If they didn't get some more food soon, they would surely collapse.

An exhausted Hansel and Gretel rested, leaning against a tree. It was early morning. "How sad," Gretel murmured. "We'll die out here, with nobody to find us."

"Don't think that way," Hansel said. But his voice had grown weary. He no longer believed his own words. He, too, could only see a terrible end.

Suddenly a white bird flew down from the sky and landed on a branch in front of them.

Sugar Candies Sprinkled All Over It.

The bird began to sing in a beautiful voice.

"She's so pretty," Gretel said. "So white. Just like Snowy."

The bird seemed to motion to Hansel and Gretel with its wing. The brother and sister got wearily to their feet. The bird took off, flying above them. It chirped, and pointed with its wing to down below.

"Look!" Hansel exclaimed, as he and Gretel came into a clearing. "It's a house. Made of food!"

Incredible as it seemed, right before them was a small house made entirely of gingerbread, with a roof made of cake and sugar candies sprinkled over all of it.

Quickly, Hansel and Gretel began eating pieces of the house. They barely cared when a voice called out,

"Nibble, nibble I hear a mouse
Who's that eating at my house?"

Stuffing their mouths with food, Hansel and Gretel replied,

"The wind, the wind, it's very mild, blowing

like a newborn child."

"Nothing like home cooking, eh?" came a cackling voice from behind them. Hansel and Gretel dropped their food and turned around. Gretel screamed and Hansel nearly choked.

An ugly old woman, leaning on a cane, hobbled toward them. She wore a long black coat that nearly covered her, and a tall pointed hat. Her hands were twisted like tree roots, and her long nails jabbed at Hansel and Gretel as she spoke in her scary, crackling voice. "You seem to like my house. Come on in and be my guests."

"We have to be on our way," Hansel said. "Our parents are expecting us."

The old lady gave Hansel a wise look. "Why would your parents leave you in the deep woods if they were expecting you?" she asked. Hansel had no answer for that. "Come inside, you have nothing to fear."

Hansel and Gretel followed the old lady inside. She made them a big meal of wonderful things they hadn't had in a long time. Then she

"Come In and Be My Guests."

took them into a room where two little beds were all made up.

"Why don't you two climb into your beds, get some rest, and we'll have a big breakfast in the morning," the woman said.

Within moments Hansel and Gretel were both sound asleep. The old lady closed the door and headed back into the kitchen.

She cackled softly. It had been at least two weeks since she had gotten any children. For the old lady really was a witch. She only pretended to be nice. Her eyes, which were very red and mean, didn't see very well. That's why she had trained the bird to find children for her. The bird led the children to the witch. The witch fed the children. Then the witch would eat the children. It never failed! She cackled again.

Early the next morning, before sunrise, the witch poked her head into the room where Hansel and Gretel were both still sound asleep. The witch quietly tapped Hansel on the shoulder. He opened his eyes.

"Come with me, boy, I have a surprise for you," she said. Hansel rubbed his eyes, got out of bed, and followed the witch outside.

"Where are we going?" Hansel asked.

"Right in here," the witch replied. She opened a gate to a small pen. Hansel walked in. The second he did, the witch slammed the gate closed from the outside, and locked it.

"What are you doing?" Hansel shouted.

"Preparing for my next meal," the witch replied. "I need to fatten you up a little, and then you'll make a tasty dinner." The witch laughed so loud, Hansel's ears started to tingle.

Hansel tried to break free, but the gate was locked solid. It was like a small jail cell. There was no getting out. Hansel banged on the walls, but it was no use. He was the witch's prisoner. There was no way to escape.

The witch went back into the house and woke Gretel by grabbing her by the hair.

"Ow!" Gretel cried. "What are you doing?"

"I'm giving you orders, little one," the witch said, her red eyes bulging. "You are to bring

"Stick Out Your Finger, Boy."

food to your brother every hour. He is to eat it. When he is plump enough, I will eat him. Now do what I say or I'll eat you right now!"

Crying and frightened, Gretel realized it was hopeless. If she ran away, the witch would eat Hansel anyway, and Gretel herself would probably be killed in the forest. If she stayed, maybe there was a chance they might somehow escape.

So for the next several days Gretel brought Hansel food that the witch made for him. Wonderful, fattening food like roast beef, chicken pies, and chocolate cakes. Meanwhile, Gretel was only allowed to eat dry cereal with no milk.

After several days of this, the witch went out to the pen to see if Hansel had gained any weight. "Stick out your finger, boy, let me see if you're getting plump," the witch demanded.

But Hansel knew the witch had poor eyesight. He had secretly kept a small bone from a chicken he had eaten. He stuck the skinny chicken bone through the pen gate.

The witch rubbed the bone. "Aiyee!" she screamed. "You're still skinny as a rail. This plan isn't working. Skinny or fat, I'm cooking and eating you tomorrow. I can't wait. I'm getting too hungry."

The next morning the witch woke Gretel early. "I'm heating the oven," she said to the little girl. "I need to see if it's hot enough to roast your brother. Take a look inside."

The witch opened the oven door and pushed Gretel toward the opening. The witch actually had grown so hungry that she'd decided to eat Gretel first, for breakfast, and then have Hansel for lunch or dinner. She was going to push Gretel into the oven, shut the door, and bake her.

Gretel paused by the oven's opening. "It's too dark in there. I can't see how to look in," Gretel said.

"You are as dumb as a goat," the witch said. "Now watch!"

The witch limped to the oven door and bent over. "See? That's all you have to do."

"Take a Look Inside."

"Oh, that looks easy," Gretel said. With that, she leaned back and then leaped forward, pushing the witch as hard as she could. The witch screamed as she fell into the oven. Gretel quickly shut the oven door and pressed it locked.

"Dumb as a goat? Or sly as a fox?" Gretel said.

Then she turned and ran outside. She found the key that opened the gate to Hansel's pen. "You did it!" Hansel shouted, as he raced out, and hugged his sister. "I knew you'd outsmart her. We're going to be all right after all!"

Brother and sister laughed and danced in a circle, holding hands. Then they went back into the witch's house. The noise from the oven had stopped. The witch was no longer screaming. She was dead.

"I saw some things here," Hansel said, "that maybe we can make use of when we get home." What Hansel had seen were huge iron boxes, all filled with diamonds, rubies, sapphires, pearls and gold. The two of them filled their pockets with all the jewels they could hold.

"Now let's see if we can't find our way home," Gretel said. They ran as fast as they could, away from the witch's house. Soon they were back in a part of the forest that looked familiar to them. Brother and sister danced for joy.

"I recognize that big tree!" Hansel said. "We're going to find our way home quickly now!"

There was still one big problem in their way. They had to cross the wide Duck River at this point. It was too far to swim across and they had no boat.

Suddenly there was a loud quacking. An enormous fluffy white duck paddled up to them. "Maybe he'll help us across," Gretel said.

"I've never spoken to a duck before," Hansel said. "You try."

"Help us, help us, Mister duck
He's Hansel, I'm Gretel, and we're stuck
We can't get over, try as we may
Won't you help us find our way?"

"That's what ducks are for! Hop aboard," the

They Hopped on the Duck's Back.

duck said.

Hansel and Gretel hopped onto the duck's back but he began to sink into the river. "Ummmf, I think we better do this one at a time," the duck said. So Hansel got off. First the duck paddled Gretel to the other side. Then he came back and carried Hansel across.

"Thank you, Mr. Duck," Gretel said. The duck quacked happily and paddled off on his merry way.

"That was fun!" cried Gretel.

"We didn't even get wet!" Hansel laughed. They made their way along the river bank, going past trees and bushes, happy knowing they were getting closer and closer to home.

The forest now looked very familiar to Hansel and Gretel. They walked for several more hours, when suddenly they came around a bend and saw their house.

The two children rushed up the front path and into the house. Their father was sitting at the table, quietly reading a book of sad poems. He had not had a happy moment since he had lost his two beloved children.

"Father, we're home!" Hansel called out. Father turned. Tears welled up in his eyes. He leaped to hug his children. "My children, you are home. It's a miracle!"

Hansel and Gretel told their father all that had happened to them, and how they had tricked the witch. Then they suddenly realized their stepmother was nowhere in sight.

"She left," Father said. "She said she'd never live a good life with me here, so she packed up and went to live somewhere else."

"Too bad for her," Hansel said. "If she'd stayed, she might have enjoyed some of this." Hansel poured all of the jewelry from his pockets onto the kitchen table. Gretel did the same. Father stared with his eyes wide open, not believing what he saw.

"See, Father, we're rich!" Gretel said, laughing and crying at the same time.

"Yes, we're rich," Father said. "But nothing makes me richer than having my two children home with me."

Hansel Poured the Jewelry onto the Table.

Father continued to go out into the forest to work, but thanks to the witch's treasure, the family never had to worry about having enough to eat ever again.

Sometimes Hansel and Gretel went with him, but they never went so deep into the forest as they had when they found the witch's house.

The children were so glad to be with their dear father again, and the family lived happily ever after.

Rumpelstiltskin

Once upon a time in a kingdom by the sea, a miller lived with his wife and their beautiful young daughter. Their home was a tiny hut just outside a village. They were so poor, that on many nights the miller and his family would go to bed hungry.

One afternoon the king was passing through the village in a horse-drawn carriage, accompanied by his many guards, servants and advisors, all on horseback.

The father, who was desperate, called out to

A Tiny Hut

the king. "Your Highness, I have a daughter who knows how to spin straw into gold!" he shouted to the king.

"Halt!" ordered the king to his driver. He leaned out the window and stared down at the unshaven, raggedly dressed miller. The king's advisors all laughed. Spin straw into gold? How ridiculous. But the king seemed quite interested.

"That is a skill I would greatly admire," the king said. "Bring your daughter to my castle tomorrow morning. I will give her a test to see if you are telling the truth." The king then ordered his carriage to move on.

A man was standing next to the miller. "Have you lost your mind?" he asked him. "Nobody can spin straw into gold. The king will punish your daughter when she is unable to do it."

The miller knew this was probably true. But he was so poor and desperate, he had to try something. Perhaps the angels would take pity on him and somehow his daughter would perform the miracle of turning straw into gold.

The next morning the miller walked his young daughter to the front gates of the king's castle.

"Father, I don't know how to spin straw into gold," she said. "The king will be very angry with me." She began to tremble and cry softly.

The miller put a comforting arm around his daughter's shoulder. "You have been a very good and brave daughter ever since you have grown up," he said. "I know somehow you will succeed at this task."

"The king is waiting for the girl!" a guard shouted out from inside the castle's gates. The father kissed his daughter on the cheek. He wiped a tear from his own eye, and then he turned and quickly walked away.

The guard opened the gate and the beautiful girl entered. She had never been in a castle before. Now here she was actually standing inside the king's own castle!

A stern voice came from behind where she stood. The girl turned. Standing there was the

A Stern Voice Came from Behind.

king. He was dressed in his royal robes and he glared at her with his blazing blue eyes.

"Follow me, young lady," he said. The king led her up several flights of stairs. He opened a door that led into a room. It had no windows, tables or chairs.

The only things in the room were a spinning wheel and huge piles of straw all around.

"Your father says you can spin straw into gold. This is your chance to prove it. I will return tomorrow morning. If you have not spun every piece of straw in this room into gold, then I will have you sentenced to death. Now begin!" the king demanded.

The king walked out, slammed the door and locked it behind him. The girl was alone in the room with the straw and the spinning wheel.

"What am I going to do?" she whispered, falling to her knees. "I cannot do this impossible chore. I will be a dead girl by tomorrow!" She started to cry aloud.

She suddenly felt a chill and for a moment the room seemed to turn dark. Then suddenly the door, which had been locked, swung open. A little man entered, and the door closed behind him.

"Who are you, and how did you get in here? The door was locked," the trembling girl said, staring at the little man. He was no more than three feet tall and dressed in strange clothes.

"It is better if I ask the questions," the dwarf said. His voice was squeaky, and when he spoke, his large red nose seemed to wiggle back and forth.

"What do you want to know?" the girl asked.

"I want to know why such a sweet young girl is crying," the little man said.

"I must spin all this straw into gold by tomorrow morning," the girl replied. "If I do not, the king will have me put to death. I am crying because I cannot do it, and tomorrow I shall be dead!"

"I'll spin it into gold for you," the dwarf said, his beady little eyes staring at her.

"You will?" the girl exclaimed. "Oh, that's wonderful! How can I ever thank you?"

"Give Me That Silver Necklace."

"You can give me that silver necklace that you're wearing around your neck."

The girl touched the necklace. It had been a gift to her from her dear departed grandmother. But she knew her grandmother would want her to be alive, so the girl removed the necklace and handed it to the little man.

He quickly put the necklace in his pocket. Then he sat down by the spinning wheel. He grabbed a handful of straw, spun it around the wheel very fast, and in moments it had turned into gold!

Then he grabbed more straw and continued to spin it into gold. The girl watched in silence as the dwarf continued to spin the straw, and heaps of gold piled up quickly.

Soon the girl's eyelids grew heavy. She fell asleep.

When she awoke, it was early morning. The dwarf was gone. So, too, was all the straw. In its place were tall stacks of gold. The door to the room opened and the king and several of his guards came in.

"This is amazing!" the king announced. "You actually can turn straw into gold."

"May I go home now?" the girl asked. She knew her father would be worried about her.

The king's eyes shone with greed. "No!" he shouted. The king had the girl taken into another room, which was even larger than the first one. It, too, was filled to the ceiling with straw.

"You have until this evening to turn all this straw into gold," the king announced. "If you do not, you will be put to death at once!"

The king and his men then left, locking the girl in the room. She moaned and cried, tears running down her cheeks.

Once again there was a whoosh of breeze in the windowless room and a slight chill ran through the girl's bones.

"I will ask for your ring this time," came a familiar voice. Standing next to her was the little dwarf. He was staring at the gold ring on the little girl's finger.

"This ring was given to me by my loving

"May I Go Home Now?"

grandmother as she lay dying," the girl said. "I promised never to part with it."

"Then you will part with your own life," the little man squeaked. "You either give me the ring, or I won't turn the straw into gold."

There was nothing the girl could do. She took off her ring, stared at it through tear-stained eyes, and handed it to the dwarf.

He quickly dropped the ring into his pocket, sat down at the spinning wheel, and again began spinning the straw into gold. The wheel spun so fast it made the girl dizzy to watch it. She closed her eyes.

When she opened her eyes hours later, the little man was gone. The entire room was filled with gold, all the way up to the ceiling.

The king and his men burst into the room. "Magnificent!" the king roared. "There is one more room filled with straw. You will turn it all into gold tonight, and after you have done that, I shall reward you."

"How?" asked the girl.

"I shall make you my wife," the king said,

touching the gold. "You shall become the queen of this realm." He turned to his servants. "Take her to the large room so she may begin at once!"

As the terrified girl was led away, the king laughed. "She may only be a miller's daughter," he said to one of his advisors, "but she's made me the richest man on earth!"

The girl was led into the huge room. It was bigger than the first two rooms put together. There was more straw in this room than she had ever seen in her life. The servants closed the door and locked it behind them.

Again, there was the rush of air and her skin turned ice cold for a moment. The dwarf was standing next to the spinning wheel.

"What will you give me this time to spin the straw into gold?" he asked.

"I have no more jewelry," the girl whimpered. "You have taken all that I have."

"There is one thing you can give me," the dwarf said.

"What is that?" asked the girl.

"You Have Done Well, My Dearest."

"A promise," he replied.

"A promise?" she asked, both surprised and worried. "What could I possibly promise you?"

"You promise me that if I spin all this straw into gold that you will give me your first born child when you become queen."

The girl stared at the strange little man. Give him her baby? At this moment having a child was the last thing on her mind. Staying alive was her only concern.

"Yes," she said. "If the king marries me, and I give birth to a baby, you have my promise I will give you the child."

With the promise given, the dwarf sat down at the spinning wheel, and soon what had been straw began being turned into pure gold.

The next morning the king entered the large room. He could not believe his eyes. There was more gold in this room than anywhere else in the entire world.

"You have done well, my dearest," the king said, taking the beautiful girl's hand in his. "I am very pleased."

The wedding was held the next evening. It was a large and grand affair. The people of the kingdom danced, dined, laughed, and were stunned at the gold that adorned every corner of every room of the castle.

Exactly one year later, the young queen gave birth to a baby boy. By now she had completely forgotten about the little dwarf and the promise she had made to him.

The queen was in her room, cradling her new baby in her arms, when she felt a rush of air and a cold chill filled the room.

"I'll take that baby now," came a squeaky voice from below. "He belongs to me."

The queen stared down. Standing near the foot of her bed was the dwarf. The promise! Suddenly, the young queen remembered.

"Oh no, please, you mustn't," the queen said. "I'll give you anything else you ask. Gold, money, diamonds, horses, land, anything. But please, do not take my darling baby from me."

The queen began to cry. Now, the dwarf was a mysterious fellow, but he had feelings. He

Cradling Her New Baby

understood how badly the young queen felt about giving up her baby.

"I will make a deal with you," the dwarf said. "I'll give you a chance to keep your baby. If you can guess my name within the next three days, then you may keep your baby, and I will disappear from your life forever. But if you cannot guess my name, then the baby is mine."

The queen realized she had no choice but to accept the dwarf's offer. "I will return tomorrow," the little man said. "Let us see if you've guessed my name by then."

The dwarf left. The queen immediately began to go over names in her mind. She called in her maids and servants and asked them to make lists of men's names.

The next day the dwarf returned. "Well?" he asked. "What do you think my name is?"

"Is it Kaspar?" she asked. The little man shook his head no. "Is it Melchior? Balzar? Therig?" To each name, the dwarf shook his head no.

"That's all for today," he said. "I'll return

tomorrow. You have only two days left to guess my name."

The queen sent her servants out into the villages and countryside to ask people for names. By the time the dwarf returned on the second day, the queen had a long list.

She began to read off the names. "Ribsobeef?" she asked. "Beefstew? Muttonchops? Spindlewheel? Strawman?"

To each name the little man shook his head no. "That's all the guesses you get today," he said. "I'll return tomorrow. Remember, tomorrow is your third and final day to guess my name."

The queen stayed up all night, trying to come up with new, unusual names that might fit the little man. While she was making her list, one of her servants entered her chamber.

"Your ladyship, I have seen a strange thing," he reported. "I was climbing one of the far mountains, looking for anyone who might know the name of the strange dwarf. I approached a cottage, and saw a fire burning

"I Saw a Strange Thing."

outside it. A weird little man was dancing around the fire and singing:

"Today I'll brew, tomorrow I'll bake,

Soon I'll have the queen's namesake.

Oh, how hard it is to play my game

When Rumpelstiltskin is my name."

The queen was so relieved and overjoyed that she gave the servant two pounds of gold as a reward. Then she fell into a restful sleep, and waited for the light of day.

The next morning the queen awoke. The curtains in her chamber swayed to a silent breeze and a chilling numbness passed through the queen. She knew the dwarf had arrived.

"Today is the third day," he said in his squeaky little voice. "Guess my name, or I leave with your baby."

The queen bit her lip. "Is it Kunz?" she asked.

"Not even close," the dwarf replied.

"Could it be Heinz?"

"No," said the little man, who was now by the bed, leaning over and reaching to pick up the little baby.

"Then I'll try one last name," the queen said. "If I'm wrong, then my dear baby is yours."

"I'm waiting," said the dwarf, his hands now almost touching the baby.

"I'm guessing your name is Rumpelstiltskin," the queen said, smiling at the dwarf.

He spun around, his face filled with disbelief. "The devil told you, the devil told you!" he shouted, and he stomped his foot down so hard it went clear through the floor. He screamed out in anger, grabbed his other foot with both his hands, and in a fit of rage, tore himself completely in half. Then he disappeared.

The queen hugged her baby in her arms, and knew that now she and her family would live happily ever after.

In a Fit of Rage

Little Red Riding Hood

Once upon a time in a small village near a large forest, a mother lived in a cottage with her young daughter.

The girl was very pretty and was the nicest girl in the entire village. Everyone loved her. But no one loved her more than her grandmother, who lived in her own cottage on the other side of the forest.

Grandmother loved the girl so much that she made her a red cape with a hood for a birthday present. The little girl loved the red cape and wore it almost every day. Soon everyone in the village began calling her Little Red Riding Hood, because she wore it all the time.

One morning Little Red Riding Hood's mother called her into the kitchen. "I've gotten news that your grandmother isn't feeling well," her mother said. "So I've baked some bread and made some apple cider I want you to bring to her. It might make her feel better."

"Oh, I'm sorry grandmother's not well, but I'm happy I'll get to see her," Little Red Riding Hood said.

"I'll put the bread and cider in a basket," her mother said. "You are to go straight through the forest and go directly to grandma's house," she added. "You are not to stop and play, and by no means are you to talk to any strangers. Do you understand?"

"Yes, Mother," Little Red Riding Hood replied sweetly. Soon she was out of the door, with the basket in her hand, and skipping into the path that led through the forest.

Little Red Riding Hood loved the forest. She

Little Red Riding Hood Jumped Around.

loved how the sun's rays shone through the branches of the trees. She loved the colors and sweet smells of the flowers and plants that grew all around. She smiled at the little birds and animals that romped through the bushes. She laughed as a little squirrel came up to her and said, "Good morning."

"Good morning to you, Mr. Squirrel," she replied, and tossed him a nut she had in her pocket. The squirrel ran happily up a tree and ate the nut.

"You are a very kind little girl," a voice suddenly thundered from behind her.

Little Red Riding Hood jumped around, startled. She nearly dropped her basket. She was staring at a large wolf!

Now, she had heard that wolves are dangerous and will eat people when they are hungry. But this wolf seemed very friendly. He was also dressed in a fine jacket, fancy hat and leather gloves.

"I like the forest animals," Little Red Riding Hood replied, as the wolf stepped from behind a tree and approached her.

"Did you come to play here?" the wolf asked.

"No," she replied. "I'm on my way to visit my grandmother, who isn't feeling well."

"I'm sorry to hear that," said the wolf. "Where does your grandmother live?"

"Just on the other side of the forest," Little Red Riding Hood replied. "The first cottage beneath three large oak trees."

"I see," said the wolf. He stared at her basket. "Are you bringing your sick grandma something to eat?"

"Yes," Little Red Riding Hood replied. "Some bread and apple cider."

"That's very nice," said the wolf. "But maybe you should bring her some flowers, too. Look at all these lovely purple flowers growing by the side of the path."

Little Red Riding Hood looked at the flowers by the path. They were truly beautiful. She had never seen any flowers as beautiful as these. They would make a lovely gift for Grandma.

A Lovely Gift for Grandma

"That's a good idea," Little Red Riding Hood said. "I think I will pick some and bring them to Grandmother."

"Glad I could be of help," the wolf said, bowing and tipping his cap. "I must be off now. I have work to do. I hope your grandmother feels better."

The wolf turned and darted off into the woods. Little Red Riding Hood bent down and began to pick several of the purple flowers from the ground.

As she placed the flowers in her basket, she remembered what her mother had said about not talking to strangers. But the wolf had been very nice, nothing like the scary stories Little Red Riding Hood had heard about wolves. She continued to pick the flowers and hummed a happy tune.

Meanwhile, the wolf was racing as fast as he could through the forest. He chuckled. "What a foolish little girl," he said to himself. "She not only tells me where her grandmother lives, but she then lets me trick her into staying in the forest so I can get to grandmother's house first. The two of them shall make a delicious meal."

The wolf licked his lips with his thick tongue. A few moments later he came to the edge of the forest. Beneath three oak trees stood a small cottage. The wolf knocked on the front door.

"Who's there?" called out a weak, old voice from inside.

"It's me, Grandma," replied the wolf, doing his best to imitate Little Red Riding Hood's voice.

"Little Red Riding Hood, my darling girl!" replied the old woman. "Come in. Open the latch. I'm in the bedroom."

The wolf lifted the latch, entered the house and closed the door behind him. He dashed into the bedroom. The old grandmother had struggled to her feet, near her bed. She stared wide-eyed at the wolf.

"You're not my granddaughter!" she screamed.

"But you will be my lunch," the wolf replied,

Grandmother's Cottage

laughing. The old lady closed her eyes and fainted to the floor.

"I'll eat you later," the wolf said. "I must quickly prepare for my visitor." So the wolf dragged the grandmother to a closet in the bedroom, opened the door, and shoved her inside.

Then he took a long nightgown and sleeping cap out of the closet. He closed the closet door and locked it, with the poor old grandmother slumped inside.

The wolf quickly changed into the nightgown and cap, got into the bed, and pulled the covers up to his chin. He laughed. "I haven't had a good meal in nearly a week," he said. "Today I shall have a feast!"

Moments later there was a knock on the front door. "Who's there?" the wolf called out, doing his best to imitate the grandmother's voice.

"Grandma, it is Little Red Riding Hood."

"Oh my dear girl, open the latch and come in. I'm in the bedroom," the wolf called out weakly.

Little Red Riding Hood opened the door, entered the cottage, and came eagerly into her grandmother's bedroom. She took one look at Grandma and was startled. Grandma must truly be sick; Little Red Riding Hood had never seen her look as she did now.

"I've brought you some bread and cider Mother made," she said. "I've also brought you some beautiful flowers I found in the forest."

"Oh, they're lovely," the wolf said. "Bring them closer so I can see them better, my dear."

Little Red Riding Hood approached the bed. Now she got an even better look at her grandmother. She was amazed at how odd Grandma looked.

"Grandmother, what big eyes you have," Little Red Riding Hood said.

"The better to see you with, my dear," the wolf replied, his voice almost cracking as he tried to imitate the old woman.

Then Little Red Riding Hood noticed something that truly startled her. "Grandmother, what big ears you have!"

How Odd Grandma Looked.

"The better to hear you with, my dear," the wolf said. "But you must come even closer, so I can see and hear you better."

Feeling something was terribly wrong, Little Red Riding Hood slowly approached the bedside. She stared down at her grandmother's face.

"Grandma," she said, "what big teeth you have!"

"The better to eat you with, my dear!" shouted the wolf. He suddenly jumped up, ripped off the bedclothes, and leaped at Little Red Riding Hood.

The girl screamed, and ducked under a chair, as the wolf began chasing her around the room. She screamed and screamed as loudly as she could.

Luckily, at that moment, there was a woodsman chopping some trees nearby the cottage. He heard the cries coming from the house. With his hatchet in his hand, he ran into the house and burst into the bedroom.

"Help me, please, he's going to eat me!" Little Red Riding Hood called out.

"Oh no, he won't!" yelled the woodsman. Using his hatchet like a hammer, he slammed it twice against the wolf's forehead.

The wolf let go of Little Red Riding Hood, and he fell to the floor.

"Thank you, you saved my life!" Little Red Riding Hood cried, hugging the woodsman.

"I'm glad I was here," he replied. "That wolf has been tricking people for a long time. Now he'll never do it again."

Suddenly Little Red Riding Hood screamed again. "What is it?" asked the woodsman.

"My grandmother!" she replied. "This is her house. I came here because she was ill. Where is she? Grandma!" Little Red Riding Hood yelled out, spinning and looking all around.

There was a faint banging from inside the closet door. "Help me, please," came the faint voice of the old woman.

"Grandma!" Little Red Riding Hood shouted,

The Three of Them Sat Down.

running to the closet. She turned the knob. It wouldn't open. "It's locked!" she cried.

"Stand back," said the woodsman. He lifted his hatchet and with one mighty stroke split open the closet door. The woodsman reached inside and helped Grandmother out of the closet.

"Grandma, are you all right?" Little Red Riding Hood asked, hugging her.

"I'm a little dizzy, but I'll be fine now, dear girl," she said, hugging her granddaughter and smiling at the woodsman.

Then the three of them sat down at the kitchen table and ate the bread and drank the apple cider. Little Red Riding Hood told them about how she had met the wolf in the forest, and how sorry she was about poor Grandma's fright. "I hope I get to visit you many more times, Grandma," Little Red Riding Hood said.

"You will, my dear," she replied. "But remember, in the future, never ever to stop and speak to strangers."

"Especially if they're wolves," the woodsman added.

"Most especially if they're wolves," echoed Little Red Riding Hood's grandmother.

Little Red Riding Hood agreed to that, and she did make many more visits to her grandmother's house, and they all lived happily ever after.

Many More Visits

Rapunzel

Once upon a time in a land of hills and gardens, a husband and wife lived in a small snug cottage.

They were good people and they got along with everyone in the local village. They had everything they needed in their lives, except for one thing. They had no children.

Then one day the wife came home, smiling happily. "Wonderful news!" she told her husband. "I am going to have a baby!"

They were so happy they hugged and

laughed. They started thinking of what to call the baby. The next day the wife spent the whole morning thinking of possible names. She stared out the back window of their house, into the garden down below.

Her eyes opened with amazement. She realized she was staring at a bed of the most beautiful, tempting turnips she had ever seen. They were full, ripe and she was aching to eat one.

Her desire to eat the turnips became so great that she refused to eat any other food, and she began to grow pale and weak.

Her husband was very concerned. "What's wrong, my darling?" he asked. "We are going to have a baby soon, and you should be eating and keeping yourself healthy."

"I will not be happy until I have those turnips from the garden below," the wife said. "If I don't have some, I know I will die."

The husband was terrified. He knew it was very important for his wife to eat something soon or she and their coming baby would both die. But no one had ever gone into that garden

The Husband Climbed the Wall.

before, because it was the property of an evil old witch. If she caught anyone in her garden, the rumors were that she did terrible things to them.

But this was an emergency. So, early that evening, the husband climbed the wall and jumped down into the witch's garden. He quickly uprooted several turnips, ran back to the fence, climbed back over it, and went upstairs.

His wife was overjoyed. "These turnips are so beautiful!" she said. She quickly chopped them up, and cooked them, and she and her husband ate them for dinner.

"They were good," the husband said, finishing the meal. "Now are you happy?"

"For this one night," the wife said. "But tomorrow I will need even more. I must have more turnips!"

The husband moaned. He would have to risk his safety again tomorrow, and bring back more turnips. The following afternoon, he again leaped over the fence, and started pulling turnips from the ground.

"So you are the turnip thief," cackled an angry voice from behind him. Startled, the husband turned. The ugliest woman he had ever seen was staring at him. She had hardly any teeth, her skin was wrinkled, her eyes were yellow and they didn't blink. "I shall now punish you for your crime," she said, as she prepared to place a curse on the husband.

"No, please, forgive me," he said, falling to his knees. "I only took the turnips because my wife, who is soon to give birth to a child, said she would die if she could not eat some of your turnips."

The witch paused. Her anger eased. "That is different," she said. "In that case, you may take as many turnips as you wish."

"Thank you," said the husband, getting to his feet.

"I have one demand, however," added the witch.

"A demand?" asked the husband. He knew the witch was about to say something that

"Take as Many as You Wish."

would be terrible.

"Yes," said the witch. "In exchange for the turnips, you are to give me your child as soon as your wife gives birth. I will take care of it as if I were its true mother." The husband was shocked. But his wife would die without the turnips. So he had no choice but to agree to the witch's demand.

A few weeks later, the wife gave birth to a beautiful little girl. The witch arrived in the middle of the night and took the baby away.

"I shall call you Rapunzel," the witch said to the baby girl in her arms. The witch chuckled. She was laughing because the turnips the wife had craved were called Rapunzel turnips, so Rapunzel was a fitting name for the child.

As time passed, Rapunzel grew to become the most beautiful girl in the entire realm. The witch moved her to a castle far out in the countryside.

Because Rapunzel was so beautiful, the witch did not want other people to see or be around her, especially young men. So the witch made Rapunzel live in a tower that had no stairs or doors. There was only one window at the very top.

Each day, when the witch wanted to enter the tower, she would call up:

"Rapunzel, Rapunzel

Let down your hair," because Rapunzel had the most beautiful, longest hair in all the world, and it was the color of gold.

When Rapunzel heard the witch call out those words, she would unloose her braids and let her hair out through the window, the entire way down to the ground. The old hag would climb up the side of the tower, pulling on Rapunzel's hair like a rope, until she reached the window.

Rapunzel's life went on like this for the next few years. She never left the tower. She never met anyone, other than the witch. She grew more beautiful every day, but there was no one to share her beauty with.

One thing she did to keep herself busy was to sing out loud. Often the birds flying by the

He Saw the Old Witch Approach.

tower would sing back in reply.

Then one day a prince, riding on his horse, came by the tower. He passed by just as Rapunzel was singing a song about rainbows.

The prince stopped. He had never heard such a beautiful voice. He knew the singing was coming from the top of the tower, but he couldn't see any doors or openings to the building. Frustrated, he rode home to his castle. But as he slept that night, all he could dream about was the beautiful voice he had heard that afternoon.

The prince was drawn back to the tower the very next day. As he stood behind a tree, listening to Rapunzel singing about the stars and the sea, he saw the old witch approach the tower.

The witch called out her orders to Rapunzel, to lower her hair.

The prince watched in amazement as the witch climbed up the side of the tower, using Rapunzel's long, blonde hair. "So that's how a person gets into the tower," the prince said. He realized he needed a plan.

The next evening the prince returned to the tower. And using his voice to make it sound like the witch's, he called out,

"Rapunzel, Rapunzel,

Let down your hair," and in moments the blonde hair was flowing down. He grabbed it, climbed up the side of the tower, and through the window into the room.

"Who are you?" asked Rapunzel. The prince was the first man she had ever seen. In fact, he was the first person other than the old witch that she had ever seen. She was frightened, but as soon as the prince spoke to her, she calmed down.

"You have the most beautiful voice I have ever heard," he said. "You are also the most lovely girl I have ever seen. It is wrong for you to be kept in this tower like a prisoner. Let me free you. Come with me, Rapunzel, and be my wife."

Rapunzel had read books about kings and queens and princes, and she realized that this

"Come With Me, Rapunzel."

wonderful young man was a prince. She knew that with him she would be far happier than she could ever be with the ugly witch.

"I do want to be your wife," she said, taking the prince's hand in hers. "But I have to get out of this room and down to the ground."

They knew the prince could jump out of the window, because he was a prince and was used to doing such things. But Rapunzel had never done anything like that, and if she tried it she might get badly hurt.

"I have a plan!" Rapunzel said. "You must come to visit me in the evening, when the witch is away. She is only here during the daytime. Bring with you skeins and bundles of silk. When I have enough silk, I will weave it into a ladder. Then I can climb down the ladder and you can take me away on your horse."

"I will come every evening with the silk," the prince promised. "Soon you will have enough to weave a ladder and we will go off to live our lives as husband and wife."

So for the next several evenings, the prince

arrived and brought Rapunzel skeins of silk. She began to weave the ladder.

One afternoon, while Rapunzel wasn't paying attention, the witch came into the tower room. She saw Rapunzel weaving the silken ladder.

"Planning an escape, are you?" she shrieked at Rapunzel. "Is this how you repay me for taking such good care of you?"

"I am sick of being in this tower," Rapunzel said. "There is a prince who loves me very much and I love him. We wish to live our lives together, away from you and this place."

The witch was outraged. Without saying another word she grabbed a pair of shears, grasped Rapunzel's long hair, and with one snap, cut off her hair. Then she had Rapunzel taken away, to a lonely desert where only snakes and lizards lived.

Then the witch returned to the tower. She still had Rapunzel's hair, which she had clipped off. She waited until she heard the prince call out from below:

The Witch Was Outraged.

"Rapunzel, Rapunzel,

Let down your hair," at which point the witch, having fastened the braids to hooks, let the hair down to the ground.

The prince pulled himself up to the top of the tower and entered the room. When he saw the witch standing there, he gasped.

"Not who you were expecting?" the witch said, laughing with an evil cackle. She approached the prince. "Perhaps you want to marry me instead of Rapunzel?"

The prince took two steps back. "Where is my love? What have you done to her, you evil old lady?"

"Your bird was caught by the cat," the witch said, hissing. "You will never see her again. In fact, you will see nothing!"

Shocked with grief, the prince leaped out of the window. The fall did not kill him, but he landed in a bush of thorns, which pierced both his eyes. He lost his sight.

Blind and saddened, the prince wandered for many months through the land, eating nothing but roots and berries. At night he would lie on the ground, his ears straining to hear the singing of his beloved Rapunzel. But he heard nothing but the wind and the wailing of a lonely fox.

One night, when he'd decided he could no longer go on, the prince lay down, mourning the loss of his love, and planning to end his life.

Suddenly, from a distance, he heard a voice. Singing a song about sunsets and angels. The prince stood up. He couldn't believe it. It was his Rapunzel!

Though blind, he ran through the woods as fast as he could, getting closer and closer to the voice.

Rapunzel was sitting, alone, atop a small hill. She looked up. She could not believe her eyes. Her prince had found her!

"My love!" she called out. "Do you not see me? Here I am!"

The prince ran to the sound of her voice. He reached her and the two of them embraced. They laughed and cried. Two of Rapunzel's

He Reached Her and They Embraced.

tears touched the prince's eyes. Instantly, his eyes opened.

"I can see again!" he shouted. They hugged and gazed into each other's eyes. Then the prince led Rapunzel out of the desert, back to his kingdom, where they were welcomed with great joy by all the people. They were married in a royal ceremony, and as prince and princess lived happily ever after.

The Golden Goose

Once upon a time in a small village in a kingdom filled with many forests, a mother and father lived with their three sons.

The oldest boy was quite smart. The middle one was of normal intelligence. The youngest son was considered to be so slow that his nickname was Simpleton.

One sunny afternoon the oldest son asked his parents if he could go into the forest to chop some wood. "You're smart enough to go out on your own now," the father said. "I'll make you a

"Could I Share Your Lunch?"

nice lunch to take with you," added the mother.

So the oldest boy went off, carrying his hatchet and a sack containing a loaf of bread and a jar of lemonade.

Soon he reached a tree that looked perfect for cutting. But before he could start chopping, a little old man appeared at his side. The man was the size of a dwarf. He had a gray beard, gray eyes and even his skin looked gray.

"I haven't eaten or drunk anything in days," the dwarf said. "Could I share some of your lunch?"

The oldest son thought himself no fool. He realized if he gave this dwarf part of his lunch, he wouldn't have enough for himself.

"Sorry, old man," the boy said. "I'm afraid you'll have to find your lunch somewhere else. Leave me alone. I've got work to do."

The dwarf nodded and wandered off. The boy then cut into the tree with his hatchet. A piece of wood flew off the tree and cut the boy's arm. He immediately started to bleed. He packed up his bag, turned around, and went home to have his arm bandaged. He didn't realize that the dwarf was watching him from behind a tree, and had caused the accident to happen.

The next morning the middle son asked his father if he could go into the woods and chop down a tree. "Yes," the father replied. "But be careful, we don't want you getting hurt like your older brother did."

"Don't worry, I'll be fine," the son said. His mother made him a lunch of cornbread and goat's milk. The middle son then went out into the woods.

Before long he reached the same tree his older brother had been at yesterday. He was about to start chopping the tree, when a voice called out. "Could I have a bite to eat? I'm really hungry. I haven't eaten in days."

The boy looked down. That same gray dwarf, who had spoken to his older brother, was standing there. "The more you eat, the less I'll have," the boy responded. "Sorry, I can't help you. Now leave me alone."

The dwarf nodded, and walked off. The boy

He Was About to Start Chopping.

then whacked the tree with his hatchet. A branch immediately fell off, hitting him on the foot. The boy cried out in pain, and had to limp all the way home. As he limped off, he didn't realize the dwarf was watching him from behind a bush, and that he had caused the accident to happen.

The following morning the youngest son went to his father. "Can I go into the woods and chop down a tree?" Simpleton asked.

The father laughed. "Your brothers, who are much smarter than you, couldn't do it. How do you think you possibly can?"

"Please let me try," Simpleton pleaded. "I know I can do it."

Simpleton kept pestering his father to let him go. "Oh, let him go already," the mother said. "Maybe after he's hurt himself, he'll learn something from it."

The father agreed. He gave Simpleton an old rusty hatchet. The mother gave him a lunch of stale pancakes and a bottle of warm water to drink.

Simpleton didn't even realize he wasn't getting a meal as good as his older brothers had. He was happy just to have the chance to go out into the woods by himself.

He soon came to the tree his older brothers had reached. He lifted the rusty hatchet and was about to cut into the tree when a voice called out. "Please give me something to eat and drink or I'm afraid I may die."

Simpleton looked down. A sickly looking gray dwarf stood nearby. "I have only some stale pancakes and warm water," Simpleton said to the dwarf. "But you're welcome to join me if it'll help you."

"Thank you, young man," the dwarf said. The two of them sat down near the tree and began eating the pancakes. They washed them down with the warm water.

"You have a good heart," the dwarf said, when they'd finished all the food and drink. "You gave me something to help me. Now I want to give you something to help you. Do you see that tree with the yellow leaves?"

A Large Tree

The dwarf pointed to a large tree down the path. Simpleton nodded. "Go and chop it down," the dwarf said. "When you've finished, look at its roots. You will find something very interesting waiting there."

Simpleton stared at the tree again. When he looked back to ask the dwarf what was in the roots, the dwarf had suddenly, mysteriously vanished.

"Well, I guess I'll just have to chop it down and find out for myself," Simpleton said. So he went over to the yellow-leafed tree and began hacking away.

The tree was large and thick, and Simpleton's hatchet was old and rusty, so it took some time before he could cry "Timber!" and the tree fell to the ground.

When it did, Simpleton bent down and stared at the tree's roots. A goose suddenly popped out of the roots and into Simpleton's arms. But it was unlike any goose Simpleton had ever seen before. It was the color of pure gold. All of its feathers were golden, even its tail. Simpleton petted the goose and talked gently to him.

By now it had grown late in the day, so Simpleton decided he'd better find a place to spend the night instead of going home.

He walked to an inn he knew was in that part of the woods. When Simpleton walked into the inn, the innkeeper took one look at the golden goose Simpleton was carrying and welcomed the boy with open arms.

The innkeeper had three daughters. They came running to the front when they heard a boy had arrived at the inn carrying a golden goose.

Everyone acted very nicely toward Simpleton, but what they all really wanted was to get their hands on that golden goose and its precious feathers.

Simpleton was given one of the finest rooms in the inn. Since it was a beautiful night, and there was a full moon, Simpleton decided to go outside and look at the moon shine through the trees in the woods.

Everyone Acted Nicely to Simpleton.

The moment Simpleton stepped outside the inn, the oldest of the three daughters went into Simpleton's room. "Where are you, goose?" she said aloud. There came a honking noise from under the bed.

The girl picked up the goose. "All I want is one of your feathers," she said. "That should be enough to buy me several dresses and a necklace." She tried to pluck a feather from the goose's left wing. But when she tried to pull it off, it wouldn't budge. She tried again. Still, the feather wouldn't come off.

The girl placed the goose on the floor and turned to leave the room. But her hand was stuck to the goose's wing. She tried to let go, but hard as she tried, she couldn't let go of the goose's wing. She was stuck to the goose!

At that moment the second sister came into the room. "It seems we both had the same idea," the second sister said, touching her older sister on the shoulder.

"The oddest thing has happened," the older sister said. "I tried to pluck a feather from the goose, but it wouldn't come off. And now it seems stuck to my hand. I can't let go of the goose's wing."

"Let me try," the second sister said. She was going to pluck a feather, but when she tried to take her hand off her sister's shoulder, she suddenly realized she couldn't. "My hand's stuck to your shoulder!" she shouted.

At that moment the third and youngest of the sisters came into the room. "I want to get a golden goose feather too," the third sister said.

But before the two older sisters could warn her, the third sister put her hand on the second sister's elbow. Instantly, she found she couldn't remove her hand from the elbow.

Soon, Simpleton returned to his room. He was surprised to find the three sisters in his room, but he accepted their explanation that they were just there to watch the goose so that nothing bad would happen to it.

The next morning Simpleton woke up. He was in a hurry to get home with his golden

He Zigged, He Zagged.

goose to show to everyone.

Simpleton left the inn, with the three sisters attached to each other, and the oldest one still attached to the goose.

Simpleton placed the goose under his arm, and began to run home. He zigged, he zagged, he raced up hills, he jumped over fences, and as he did the three sisters had to run, jump and leap to keep up with him!

By now they had reached the middle of a grassy field. The local parson was passing by, on his way to church. He saw the three girls racing along with Simpleton. The parson thought the girls were being naughty, chasing after the boy.

"Shame on you, young ladies, where are your manners?" he called out. The parson reached out to stop the girls. He touched the sleeve of the third sister. Suddenly he found he couldn't let go. He was stuck too!

Now Simpleton had three sisters and a church parson attached to his golden goose. He continued racing across the field. The parson was breathing hard, trying to keep up as he was pulled along.

To the parson's distress, the church sexton came walking toward them. The sexton stared in disbelief as the group came running toward him.

"What's going on here?" the sexton yelled. "Parson, where are you going? We have a christening to perform today."

The sexton reached out to grab the parson by his coattail. He no sooner grabbed the parson's coat then he realized he couldn't let go!

So now Simpleton had five people attached to his golden goose, which he continued to cradle in his arms. The goose honked happily as Simpleton raced along, with the five others gasping to run along and keep up.

At this point two farmers came out of a nearby stable. "You, farmers, come here, fast, and cut us loose!" the sexton yelled out.

The farmers came racing over. "No," yelled the oldest sister to the farmers, "it won't do any good. Don't touch the sexton!"

"We Have a Christening to Perform!"

"What do you know, girl?" asked one of the farmers. The two farmers reached out to pull the sexton free. But they found their hands were suddenly attached to the sexton's shirt collar. They couldn't let go. Now the goose had seven people in his procession!

Simpleton kept racing along. Soon he ran down a hill into a land that was ruled by a king with a very unhappy daughter.

The daughter, who was a princess, had not laughed once in her entire laugh. She was the grimmest, most serious girl who had ever lived. The king had issued a decree that whoever could make his daughter laugh would marry her and become prince and heir to the throne.

Simpleton didn't know about any of that, but as soon as the princess saw Simpleton, the goose, and the seven people running along like dogs on a leash, she burst out into happy laughter.

"We've found our prince!" the king yelled. The king came running down and stood in the path, blocking Simpleton's way. Simpleton and the group came to a halt.

"Congratulations, young man, you're going to marry my daughter."

Behind Simpleton, the others were all yelling for help, screaming for someone to cut them loose.

All these antics only made the princess laugh even harder. But the king really didn't want a Simpleton for a son-in-law.

"Before you can marry my daughter," he said, "you must bring me a ship that can sail on land as well as on water."

The king knew this was an impossible demand. No ship could do that. Simpleton thought for a moment, and said, "I'll be right back."

He raced into the woods. He found the gray dwarf, sitting by that tree, waiting for him. "I know why you're here," the dwarf said. "When I needed food and drink you helped me. Since then, I have been helping you. I will not stop now. I will help you win the hand of the

Sails on Top and Wheels on the Bottom

princess and surprise the foolish king."

The dwarf snapped his fingers. Instantly, wood from the trees around them shaped themselves into the strangest, oddest contraption Simpleton had ever seen.

It had sails on board the top, and wheels along the bottom. It had all sorts of devices and compasses and instruments on board. The most important thing was, it could move on both land and water.

The dwarf and Simpleton hopped aboard, and began traveling down the path, toward the king's village.

Soon they approached the king's castle. Villagers laughed and applauded when they saw Simpleton aboard the strange ship. "Care to go for a ride, your highness?" Simpleton asked the king. He helped the king aboard.

Then Simpleton and the dwarf, with the king as their passenger, took the vehicle on a journey through the village, down the roads, over the paths, and finally into the giant lake just outside the village. Then they returned to the castle.

Watching all this, the princess laughed even harder than she had before. She was truly in love with Simpleton. The villagers all cheered. The king knew he was defeated.

"Very well, you may marry my daughter," the king said, getting down off the ship. Everyone in the village cheered and applauded as Simpleton and the princess kissed. The wedding took place the next evening. Simpleton and his bride moved into a smaller castle, with a special room set aside for their pet golden goose, and they all lived happily ever after.

The Wedding Took Place Next Evening.

The Princess and the Pea

Once upon a time a king and queen lived in a quiet land with their son, Prince Toringarde. The people loved the royal family, but the prince was not happy.

"I am so sad," he said to his parents. "I want to get married, but I can't find the right one for me."

"This can easily be arranged," the king said. "As many as fourteen princesses live within a one-day horse ride of our castle."

"I've met all of those girls," Toringarde said,

"but they're not truly princesses. They don't have that special royal quality I want my wife to have."

Comments like those made the queen cry, because she wanted her son to be happy, and married, and produce a grandchild for her.

"I know what I'll do," the king said. "I'll issue a written proclamation. It will state that you are looking to get married, and all true princesses may come and meet you in person. That way you will meet all the eligible girls in all of the lands."

So the king had the proclamation written, printed, and posted everywhere. Over the next several weeks many princesses came to the castle to meet Prince Toringarde.

But not one of them moved his heart. None of them had the special quality he was looking for. The experience only made the prince sadder, but the queen would not let herself lose hope.

"You will see, my son," she said. "Just when you think that it is impossible, something will

Prince Toringarde

Sadly Thinking in His Chamber

happen. It could be just outside our front door. The trick is to know how to look for what you are seeking."

The prince thought his mother was just trying to make him feel better. He didn't really believe her words. If a princess existed who was right for him, she would have come to the castle by now.

As the prince was sitting in his chamber sadly thinking all this over, he heard a loud howling outside. He leaped to his feet and ran into the main hallway.

The king, queen, and all the servants had gathered. "What's going on?" Prince Toringarde asked.

"There is a terrible storm blowing outside," the king replied. "Winds, hail, lighting, thunder. We have never seen anything like it before in our realm."

At that moment there was a loud beating on the front door. "The wind is trying to knock the front door down," a servant cried.

"No," said Toringarde, placing his hand on

his sword. "That is not the wind. That is a human hand beating on the door. I'll go see who it is."

Everyone watched as Prince Toringarde headed toward the front door. He may have been lonely, his heart maybe breaking for lack of love, but he was still a brave, valiant prince. With his sword now drawn, he carefully opened the front door.

Standing in the doorway was a young girl, sopping wet. Prince Toringarde stared at her. "Who are you?" he asked.

"I am Princess Annasara," she replied, "and if you don't ask me in, I shall drown any second in this downpour."

The prince moved aside and the princess entered. "I was traveling back to my kingdom when the storm broke out," she said, as she was introduced to the king, queen, and all of the court.

The princess began telling how she had become trapped in the fierce winds and rain. As she spoke, her hair and her clothes began to

"I Was Travelling When the Storm Broke."

dry. Prince Toringarde saw that she was a truly beautiful princess. Also, her voice was honest and fair, and her eyes were the deepest he had ever seen. This must be the woman his mother had meant was waiting right outside the front door for him.

"Not so fast, my son," the queen said, when the prince whispered this to her. "We need to determine if she is indeed a real princess, and one who can make you happy for your whole life."

"How can we do that?" he asked his mother.

"Just leave it to me," she said. Then she turned to Princess Annasara. "May I lead you to your bedroom, my dear?" the queen asked. The storm was still raging, and the princess would have to stay overnight.

"I would be honored, your grace," the princess replied, curtseying.

"Fine. I'll go up and see that your room is prepared. I'll call you when it's ready." The queen then headed up the staircase and she entered a bedroom.

The queen took a tiny green pea out of her pocket. She placed it beneath the mattress on the bed. Then she ordered her servants to place twenty more mattresses on top of the first mattress. The very top mattress nearly reached the ceiling of the room.

"Princess Annasara, your room is ready!" the queen announced.

The princess rose from her seat. "Perhaps I'll see you in the morning," she said to the prince.

"It is my fondest hope," the prince replied. The princess then climbed the staircase.

She entered her bedroom. She gasped when she saw all the mattresses on the bed.

The queen smiled. "I wish for you to be as comfortable as possible," the queen said.

The princess thanked the queen. Then she climbed up until she reached the top mattress. She slipped beneath the sheets and closed her eyes.

"Pleasant dreams," the queen said. "After such a difficult journey, you must be very tired." The queen closed the door behind her

"That Was the Hardest Mattress."

and went back downstairs.

By dawn, the storm had ended. The sun was rising over the far hills. The queen rose and went to Princess Annasara's bedroom. The queen went in.

The princess was pacing back and forth, her hand rubbing the spine of her back.

"My dear, what is wrong?" asked the queen. "I thought you might still be asleep."

"I don't wish to complain, but I didn't sleep a wink all night," the princess said.

"Really?" the queen asked. "Why not?"

"Do not be insulted, your grace," the princess said, "but that was the hardest mattress I have ever slept on in my life. It has caused a great pain in my back."

The queen smiled. "You are a true princess!" she cried with delight.

"Of course I am," the princess said. "I told you that last night."

"But you had to pass the test, and you did," the queen said.

"What test?" asked Princess Annasara, still

rubbing her back.

By now Prince Toringarde had arrived at the room. "What is happening?" he asked.

"Your love is indeed a true princess," the queen said. "Last night I placed a tiny green pea at the bottom of her bed. Then I covered the pea with twenty mattresses. Only a true princess with the most delicate feelings would have felt the discomfort of that pea."

"Then you are my true princess," Toringarde said, taking Annasara's hand in his. "We met because of a storm, but our life together shall be serene happiness."

The prince was right. The queen ordered regal clothing sent to the princess's room, with jewels and robes befitting a true princess. Toringarde and Annasara were married within a month, and all agree that they lived happily ever after.

"Your Love is Indeed a Princess."

Cinderella

Once upon a time in a very wealthy kingdom, a man met a woman and they were married. The woman had been married once before, and she had two daughters. The man had also been married once before, and he had one daughter.

The man's daughter was sweet, kind and the most beautiful girl in the kingdom. The woman's two daughters were mean, jealous, very plain looking, and did all they could to make fun of their new step-sister.

"Clean the kitchen!" "Wash the dishes!" "Sweep the floor!" Those were the kinds of orders the two bad step-sisters and the step-mother gave to the man's daughter every day.

But the worst thing they made the beautiful girl do was sweep up the chimney dirt. Dark, messy cinders gathered in the fireplace. Each day when she would finish cleaning the fireplace, the cinders turned her ragged clothes and skin dirty with soot. Because of this, they started calling her Cinderella.

Cinderella would have gone to her father and complained about the way she was being treated, but the step-mother had Cinderella's father completely under her control. Besides, Cinderella was much too good to ever complain about anything. So she continued to do all the dirty housework, to wear the most ragged clothes, to sleep in the creakiest bed, and to hope that someday things would get better for her.

Meanwhile, the snooty step-sisters spent all their time buying fancy, expensive new clothes,

"A Scruffy Little Nobody."

eating the best foods, combing their hair and planning on ways to meet handsome, rich princes they could marry.

One morning big news was announced by the town crier. "The king's son is holding a two-day ball at the royal castle. All unmarried girls are invited, because the prince hopes to meet his future bride. Only the fairest in the land will become the prince's bride!" he announced.

"This is fantastic," the older step-sister said. "I'll wear my red velvet gown with the French trimming."

"I'm going in my lace petticoat," the younger one said, "and I'll add to it by wearing a diamond belt and a gold scarf."

The step-sisters immediately ordered their servants to prepare perfumes and other adornments for them. Then they turned to Cinderella.

"You will advise us on how to appear and act at the ball," the older one said. "Although you are a scruffy little nobody, you do seem to have good taste."

"Too bad you're not going to the ball," the younger one said to Cinderella. "Would you like to go?"

Cinderella stared at her step-sisters. "Of course I would like to go," she said gently. "Who wouldn't want to meet the prince and perhaps become his bride? But I have no suitable clothes to attend such a ball."

Both the step-sisters laughed. Seeing Cinderella unhappy made them even happier.

The following week came the first night of the ball. Cinderella was ordered to help dress and brush the hair of her step-sisters. Then the step-sisters and their mother left the cottage, as a horse-drawn carriage took them away to the castle.

Cinderella, in her stained, old cleaning clothes, sat by the window and watched the carriage move off. She began to cry.

"Why are you crying, my child?" came a soft voice from behind her.

Cinderella turned around. An old woman, short and stout, was standing there.

Cinderella Was Ordered to Help.

"Who are you?" Cinderella asked in amazement. She had never seen this creature, or anyone like her, before.

"I'm your fairy godmother," the little old woman said. 'I'm here to help you." She smiled kindly, the first kindness Cinderella had received in a very long time.

"I am crying because—because..." Cinderella was too confused to say what she was really thinking.

"You are crying because your wicked stepsisters are going to the prince's ball, and you are not," her fairy godmother said.

Cinderella slowly nodded her head yes, as tears ran down her cinder-stained cheeks.

"You can go to the ball. I will arrange it," the fairy godmother said.

"How?" asked Cinderella. "I have no clothes, no one to help me, or drive me, and the ball is beginning in a few moments."

"Go to the garden and bring me a pumpkin," the fairy godmother said. Cinderella did as she was told. She came back from the yard holding a large orange pumpkin.

The fairy godmother took the pumpkin, carved out its insides, and tapped it with her magic wand. Instantly, the pumpkin turned into a large coach, with huge wheels and golden trimmings.

"Good. Now bring me six mice," the fairy godmother said. Cinderella went to the kitchen and found six mice that had been caught in the mousetraps. Each of the mice was unhurt, and eager to escape the traps.

"Place the mice on the floor," the fairy godmother said.

Cinderella did. As she placed them on the floor, the fairy godmother tapped each mouse with her wand. In a flash, each mouse was turned into a tall, handsome gray horse!

"Now you have a coach and horses to pull the coach," the godmother said.

"But who's going to drive the coach?" asked Cinderella.

"Are there rat-traps in the house?" the fairy godmother asked.

"Now One More Thing."

"There's one down in the cellar," Cinderella said, and she ran off to get it. Luckily, one large, whiskered rat had been caught in the trap, and he was unhurt, too.

The fairy godmother tapped the rat. Instantly, the rat was changed into a chubby coachman. He had a full beard, shiny uniform and a hearty laugh.

"Now one more thing," the fairy godmother said. "Go back into the garden and find me six lizards."

Cinderella dashed outside and quickly plucked six little lizards off the apple tree in the back yard. She brought them to her fairy godmother.

The fairy godmother touched each lizard with the wand. Immediately, the lizards were turned into footmen, each ready to accompany and protect Cinderella on her trip to the ball. They stood smartly on the coach, looking every which way.

"Now you are all set to go," the fairy godmother said.

"Godmother, how can I possibly go looking like this?" Cinderella asked. Her dress was soiled and torn. Her hair, hands and face were dirty.

"You are right," the fairy godmother said. She tapped Cinderella on the forehead. Instantly, Cinderella was wearing a beautiful gown of gold and lace. On her feet were perfect little glass slippers. Her hair was set with a diamond crown and her eyes and cheeks glowed with happiness

Cinderella stared at herself in the mirror, amazed at what she saw in her reflection.

"You are the most beautiful girl in the world," the fairy godmother said. "Now go to the ball and enjoy yourself. But there is one warning. You must be home by no later than twelve o'clock midnight. If you are even one minute late, the horses will return to mice, the coach to a pumpkin, the coachmen to lizards, and you will be in your rags again."

Cinderella promised to be home before midnight. She kissed her fairy godmother good-bye

Perfect Little Glass Slippers

and went off to the ball.

Many people had already arrived at the castle. Every girl in the realm was there, trying to catch the prince's eye. But so far, he hadn't seen any girl he really liked.

As the prince stared at the front gate, he saw a magnificent coach pull up. Six coachmen hopped out and opened the carriage door. Cinderella emerged from the coach. The prince almost lost his breath. He found himself nearly speechless.

As Cinderella entered the castle and headed into the ballroom, the prince followed her. All eyes turned toward Cinderella. People began to whisper. "Who is that girl? She's the most beautiful in the world."

The prince went over to Cinderella. He asked her to dance.

She smiled as the prince took her in his arms. Everyone watched as the prince and Cinderella danced to a merry tune.

When the song ended, Cinderella thanked the prince, and went over to her step-sisters, who were sitting at a nearby table. Cinderella sat down, and offered the step-sisters some oranges and peaches she had found in the coach.

The step-sisters were happy to receive the gifts from the beautiful stranger. Cinderella looked so different that even her own step-sisters did not recognize who she was! Cinderella did not tell them, but continued to sit with them and act kindly to them.

"The prince seems quite taken with you," the older step-sister said to Cinderella.

"I think he wants to dance with you again," the younger step-sister said. Indeed, the prince was standing across the room, staring at Cinderella. He was unable to take his eyes off her.

Cinderella laughed happily. She danced with the prince again and again. Each time he asked her her name or where she lived, she would gracefully change the subject.

Cinderella glanced at the clock. It was fifteen minutes before midnight. She realized she had to leave if she was going to be home on

"It Was Magnificent."

time. Cinderella slipped away from the ball-room, and had her coach take her home.

She arrived home just before midnight. Her fairy godmother was waiting for her.

"I had the most wonderful time. The prince is so handsome and good," Cinderella said. "I wish I could go back tomorrow for the second night of the ball."

The fairy godmother was about to answer when the front door opened. The two step-sisters were home. The fairy godmother instantly disappeared.

Cinderella, who was now dressed once more in her old, raggedy clothes, stretched her arms and pretended to yawn. "You were gone a long time," she said to her step-sisters. "I decided to wait up for you, to see how the ball went."

"It was magnificent," said the older step-sister. "The most beautiful princess in the world was there. I think the prince fell instantly in love with her."

"She was so nice to us," said the younger one. "She sat with us, and gave us oranges and peaches. The odd thing was, the princess left suddenly, without telling anyone her name or where she lived, or where she was going. I think the prince is heartbroken."

Cinderella pretended not to care. She yawned again and went to her small room and creaky old bed. She fell asleep with a smile on her face. She dreamed all night of the prince, and how they had danced and laughed together.

The next day the fairy godmother returned. "Please arrange for me to go to the ball again tonight, Godmother," Cinderella begged. "I must see the prince again."

"Very well," said the fairy godmother. "But remember, you must be home by midnight."

Cinderella promised. The fairy godmother tapped Cinderella on the shoulder with her wand. Instantly, Cinderella was wearing a gown even more beautiful than the one before. Her coach and attendants were waiting for her.

Cinderella soon arrived at the ball, which was again already under way. The prince was

How They Had Danced

sitting sadly on a royal throne. He had hoped the beautiful girl from last night would return, but so far she had not.

He looked up. Cinderella was standing before him. "Good evening, your grace," she said. The prince felt his heart leap with joy. He jumped to his feet and swept Cinderella onto the dance floor. Everyone in the ballroom watched as Cinderella and the prince danced to each song the royal orchestra played.

"I have never known anyone as beautiful, charming or sweet as you," the prince said, as they finished a dance.

"You are the handsomest, most wonderful man I have ever met," Cinderella said.

"Wait for me here," the prince said. "I'll go and get us some wine."

The prince went off to where the wine was being poured. Cinderella glanced at the clock. It was two minutes to midnight!

Running as fast as a deer, Cinderella dashed out of the ballroom and past the palace guards. She ran down the steps, and toward her coach.

She was in such a hurry that one of her glass slippers fell off and lay at the bottom of the steps.

Cinderella leaped into her coach and ordered the driver to take her home quickly. The prince came running down the steps. He looked all around. "Did you see a beautiful girl just leave?" he asked a guard.

"I saw a lovely girl leave in a carriage," the guard said. "She lost her slipper, she was running so fast." The guard handed the glass slipper to the prince.

Cinderella ran into her house. She was back into her old ragged cleaning dress. Shortly after, her two step-sisters came home from the ball.

They told Cinderella that the beautiful young princess had been at the ball again, but that she had once more fled in a great hurry right before midnight.

"She left so fast, she ran out of one of her glass slippers, which the prince found," the older step-sister said.

Only One Foot Would Fit the Slipper.

Cinderella went to bed, trying to sleep. But all she could think about was the prince. Would she ever be able to see him again? It was very hard to sleep that night.

The next morning, the town crier walked through the village streets, shouting, "The prince has found a glass slipper. He has ordered every maiden to try on the slipper. The maiden's foot that fits in the slipper, the prince shall marry and make her the princess of all the realm." For the prince knew that only the foot of the beautiful princess, whom he loved, would fit in the glass slipper.

An hour later there was a knock on the front door. Cinderella opened the door. A servant of the prince entered. He held the glass slipper.

"Let me try it on," said the older step-sister. She tried squeezing her foot into the slipper. But her foot was too big, and would not fit.

"Now let me try it on," said the younger step-sister. Her foot, being tiny, entered the slipper but the slipper was much too large for her foot.

"Neither of you is the maiden the prince

seeks," said the servant. He turned to leave.

"Wait!" called out Cinderella. "Let me try it on."

Both step-sisters laughed. "Look at you," said the older step-sister. "You are dirty and ragged. How could you possibly be the prince's love?"

But the servant was under orders to let every maiden try on the slipper. He held it out. Cinderella slipped it on. Her foot went in the slipper perfectly. It fit her foot as if it had been made for her.

"It is you!" cried the servant. "You are the one the prince loves and seeks!"

The two step-sisters shrieked in amazement and dismay. How could this possibly be, they wondered.

At that moment the fairy godmother appeared. She tapped Cinderella on the shoulder with her wand. Instantly, Cinderella was dressed exactly as she had been the previous night.

"It is you!" cried the older step-sister.

"It Is You!"

"Yes, it is," Cinderella said. "The prince loves me. And I love him. I shall be his bride. I also forgive both of you for treating me so badly. As princess, I will see to it that you are treated well and no harm comes to you."

The two step-sisters embraced Cinderella. They thanked her for her kindness. Then the servant led Cinderella out of the cottage and into the royal coach.

Soon, the coach reached the castle. Cinderella leaped to the ground, where the prince was waiting for her. "You look even more beautiful than ever," he said.

Two days later Cinderella and the prince were married in the royal chapel, and for the rest of their lives lived happily ever after.

Tom Thumb

Once upon a time in a little kingdom, a poor farmer and his wife lived in a tiny cottage.

One night as the farmer was husking corn off a cob, his wife began to cry in her rocking chair. "What is wrong, my dear?" the farmer asked.

"We have so little," the wife said. "This house is so sad. We have no money, no jewels, no wealth. But worst of all, we have no children."

"Yes," the farmer agreed. "It is a sad house. It is always so quiet without a child around.

"The Size of Your Thumb."

Would you like a child?"

"More than anything in the world," the wife replied. "Even a tiny baby, no bigger than my thumb, would make me happy."

A little fairy, listening outside the cottage window, heard the unhappy couple talking. They were good people, and she felt sorry for them. She decided to grant their wish, exactly as the wife had uttered it.

In due time, the wife had a little baby, but so little was he, that he measured no bigger than her thumb.

"Look at how small our baby boy is," the mother said, holding the tiny baby.

"You said you'd be happy with a baby the size of your thumb," the farmer said. "That is exactly what you got."

Because of that, the parents named their baby boy Tom Thumb. Although they fed him as much as they could, the baby did not grow very much.

But even though Tom was no larger than a thumb, he grew up bright and clever. One day

Tom overheard his father say how nice it would be if someone could drive the wagon into the forest to gather the wood he had chopped.

"I'll drive the wagon, Father," Tom said.

His father laughed. "Tom, you're not big enough to drive a butterfly, let alone a wagon."

"Yes, I can," Tom said. "Let me try it once."

So on the appointed day, his mother hitched the horses to the wagon. "Okay, Mother, now place me in one of the horse's ears," Tom said. His mother carefully placed Tom inside a horse's ear.

Tom immediately began calling out "Giddyap, go boy, go!" into the horse's ear. The horse took off.

As the wagon charged along, through the forest, two men saw it pass by. They were amazed. "That wagon is moving without a driver," said one of the men. He didn't see little Tom Thumb in the horse's ear.

The two men decided to follow the wagon, to see where it would end up.

Shortly, the wagon reached the part of the

"To Drive a Butterfly . . ."

forest where Tom's father waited with his chopped wood.

"Whoa!" Tom cried into the horse's ear. The horse and wagon came to a halt. "See, Father, I did it!" Tom called out.

"Yes, you did, Tom!" Father said, removing his son from the horse's ear. He placed Tom on a bed of straw, so he could rest. "I'm proud of you," Father said.

All this was seen by the two men who had followed the wagon. "That little boy could make us a fortune in the city," one man said to the other. "We could exhibit him in a circus. Let's buy him from his father."

They approached the farmer. "Sir, we have an offer to make," the first man said. "Sell us your little boy here, and we'll take good care of him for you."

"Not for all of the gold in all of the hills," Tom's father replied. "This is my darling son, and I would never sell him!"

But Tom Thumb thought otherwise. He hopped up onto his father's shoulder. "Father, you and Mother need the money badly. Sell me to these men, and I promise I'll find my way home to you before long."

So with Tom's blessings, the farmer sold his son to the two men for a good deal of money. Father gave Tom a loving little tap on his forehead, and the two men took Tom with them.

"We're going to be walking into town," one of the men said to Tom. "Where would you like to sit?"

"On the brim of your hat," Tom said. "That way I can enjoy the view."

So the man placed Tom on the brim of his hat, and the men started walking through the forest toward town.

In a little while, Tom called out, "Put me down, please, hurry!"

"Are you being attacked by a bee?" the man asked.

"Just put me down, hurry!" Tom repeated. The two men stopped. The one with the hat reached up, grabbed Tom, and placed him on the ground. "Now what?" asked the second man.

The Body of a Fish

"Now I say good-bye," Tom said, laughing. Before the men could grab him, Tom jumped into a mousehole. He could hear the two men up above, stamping and shouting. Tom laughed some more. He had outsmarted them.

By nightfall, the two men had left. Tom crawled out of the hole. "It's so dark out here," he said. "I'd better find a safe place to spend the night. Then I'll start on my way home in the morning."

Tom saw the body of a fish nearby. It was just the right size for him. Tom hopped into the fish, curled himself up, and closed his eyes to go to sleep for the night.

Just then, Tom heard two men's voices. "We need to get the rich pastor's money and silver," the first voice said.

"Yes, but how are we going to do it?" the second asked.

"I'll tell you how," Tom called out from the fish.

"What was that?" the men yelled, frightened.

"Who said that?"

"Just look down, and follow your ears," Tom said, climbing out of the fish. When the two would-be thieves saw Tom, they started to laugh.

"How can you help us?" the first man asked. "You're no bigger than my thumb."

"Just lead me to this pastor's room," Tom said. "Then I'll slip between the iron bars and get whatever you want."

"Why, that's worth a try," the second man said. So Tom got up, placed himself on the back of a nearby rat, and drove him to the pastor's house.

As soon as they reached the little house, Tom crawled into the pastor's room. "How much should I steal?" Tom yelled out loudly to the two men.

"Not so loud, you'll wake everybody up," one of the men whispered back.

But Tom pretended he didn't hear the whisper. "Should I take just the money, the silver, or everything?" Tom yelled back.

On the Back of a Rat

"Just start handing us stuff," the first man said.

Meanwhile, Tom's yelling had awakened the maid, sleeping in a nearby room. She climbed out of her bed and stumbled into the darkened room, where Tom was. She lit a candle.

Now the two men, seeing a candle lit, got scared, and immediately ran away. Tom ducked between the maid's feet and scrambled out into the hallway.

The maid looked around. When she saw no one, she assumed she had been dreaming. So she blew out the candle and went back to bed.

Tom ran out of the house and into the barn. His plan was to sleep on some hay in the barn, wake up in the morning, and then steal some of the pastor's gold in the daylight, when he could see better. Then he would take the gold home to his mother and father.

Tom fell asleep atop the hay. Early the next morning, however, the maid came into the barn.

"Time for breakfast," the maid said to the

cow, who was in the stall next to the hay. The maid grabbed the bundle of hay, with Tom on top of it, and fed it to the hungry cow.

Tom immediately woke up. "Where am I?" he cried out. He soon realized the terrible danger, when he saw the cow's large teeth chomping away right beside him. A moment later the cow swallowed, and Tom slid down the cow's throat, with the hay, into the cow's stomach.

"Whoa!" Tom yelled, as he rolled down inside the cow. "It's dark in here!" But Tom's biggest problem was that the hay kept coming. The more hay the cow ate, the less room there was for Tom in the cow's stomach.

The maid was milking the cow. She heard Tom's voice as he called out. "The cow is talking!" she cried. She ran back into the house and woke the pastor.

"A talking cow?" the pastor said. "That cannot be. Cows can't talk."

"Come hear for yourself then," the maid replied. So the pastor followed her into the barn.

The Cow's Large Teeth Chomping Away.

As they approached the cow, Tom cried out, "No more hay, no more hay!"

"This cow is cursed by the devil!" the pastor roared. "Kill him right away!"

So the cow was slaughtered. She was laid to rest in a field. Tom spent the entire day trying to dig his way out of the cow's stomach.

Just as Tom was about to break out of the cow's stomach, a hungry wolf came running over. He saw the dead cow and in one gulp ate up and swallowed the cow's stomach.

Now Tom was stuck inside the wolf. But Tom was as brave as he was small. "Mr. Wolf," he called out, "I know a place where you can eat a delicious meal."

The wolf stared down at his stomach. "Where is that?" he asked.

Tom gave the wolf the directions to his parents' house. By night, the galloping wolf, with Tom inside him, had arrived there.

The wolf was smart. He waited until the house was dark. Then he sneaked inside, and ate up all the chicken, bread and cake in the kitchen. The wolf was ready to leave, but he had eaten so much, and gotten so fat, that he couldn't fit through the door.

Tom had planned on that. He began to yell as loud as he could.

"Quiet!" the wolf whispered. "You'll wake the whole house up." But that was exactly Tom's plan. He continued to shout at the top of his lungs.

The noise woke Tom's parents. They tip-toed to the kitchen and peeked inside. They saw the fat wolf sitting on the floor. Father had an axe in his hand, and Mother held a knife.

"I'll go after him first," Father said. "If I can't kill him, you start."

"Father, Father!" Tom yelled out, when he heard his father's voice through the door. "I'm stuck inside the wolf's stomach!"

"It's Tom!" Mother cried.

"I'll take care of this," Father said. He slowly went into the kitchen. The wolf was now too fat to jump or attack. Father lifted his axe, and gave the wolf a whack across the head.

The wolf fell over, knocked out cold. Then Mother stabbed the wolf and Father carefully cut the wolf's stomach.

Tom popped right out! "We've been worried sick over you," Father said, hugging Tom.

"We've missed you so," said Mother, kissing the top of Tom's head.

"I'm home now," Tom said. "I've traveled the world, it's great to breathe the open air again, but best of all to see my dear parents."

Tom told them all about his adventures. "One thing is for sure," Father said. "No matter what, we will never sell you again."

The three of them hugged and cried for joy, and Tom Thumb and his family lived happily ever after.